Ramon walked slowly toward home along Columbus Avenue, trying to remember exactly what Glasser had said about his writing. *You've got something. You should write. And then write more. If something hurts, write it.* He touched his knife, then he touched the book in his other pocket.

That book was his knife, Glasser had said. But he needed his knife.

Ramon was close to his neighborhood, to Harpo's territory, but he wanted to think some more about what Glasser had said.

He headed for his secret place in the old railroad cut on Fifty-third Street. As he scrambled and skidded down the embankment toward his spot among the tires and weeds, he pushed against the hulk of an old boiler to stop his slide. The metal felt cool in the October evening.

There was a sound of gravel grinding against gravel from above. Ramon looked up. At the break in the fence, squeezing through one at a time, were Harpo, Dopey Luis, Angel, and Julio. They began scrambling and sliding down the embankment, one after the other.

Oh man. I'm dead. I'm dead. I can't take 'em all on. And I can't get past them. Think! Think! Talk to 'em! Talk!

Other Books by Myron Levoy

The Witch of Fourth Street and Other Stories
Alan and Naomi
Kelly 'n' Me

A Shadow like a LEOPARD

MYRON LEVOY

HarperTrophy
A Division of HarperCollinsPublishers

A Shadow Like a Leopard
Copyright © 1981 by Myron Levoy

Manufactured in the United Kingdom by HarperCollins Publishers Ltd.
For information address HarperCollins Children's Books, a division of
HarperCollins Publishers, 10 East 53rd Street, New York, NY 10022.

Library of Congress Cataloging-in-Publication Data
Levoy, Myron.
  A shadow like a leopard.

  Summary: A street-punk poet and an old painter form a friendship
and confront their fears.
  [1. Friendship—Fiction.]   I. Title.
PZ7.L5825Sh   1981   [Fic]   79-2812
ISBN 0-06-023816-X
ISBN 0-06-023817-8 (lib. bdg.)
ISBN 0-06-440458-7 (pbk.)

First Harper Trophy edition, 1994.

For Charlotte

1

Ramon Santiago felt the knife in his pocket, the knife that opened to a six-inch blade at the touch of a button. He could see the sweat on Harpo's face as they crouched in the dim landing. Yes, Harpo was sweating. Good, thought Ramon. I ain't the only one scared.

Harpo was sweating, but he knew what he was doing. He had darkened the landing by unscrewing the bare light bulb. Ramon had admired that, had admired the way Harpo had licked his fingers before touching the hot bulb.

"When's she coming, Harpo? I bet she ain't never coming," Ramon whispered. "She took all her Social Security money and she's gone on a trip to Bermuda, right?"

"Shut up, man," Harpo whispered back. "If you

can't wait, you're no good for nothing. You gotta learn to wait."

Ramon stared at the apartment door a flight below. Old lady, he thought, be big and fat. I don't wanna steal nothing from no skinny ladies.

From the half-open window, Ramon heard the up-and-down braying of a distant police car. "Hey, that's good," he whispered. "Yeah. 'Cause if they're *there*, then they ain't *here*. Keep going, police! Right on into the Hudson River. Catch yourself some big, slimy Hudson River eels. Catch yourself a dead stiff weighed down with cement blocks. Catch yourself a load of New York garbage and—"

"Hey, Santiago," whispered Harpo. "Don't you never shut up? All day long, all you do is make up that crazy bull."

"It's practice," said Ramon. "Like if you're gonna be a wrestler, you pump iron, right? If you're gonna be, like, a TV writer, you make stuff up. Yeah, that's it; it's practice."

"You ain't gonna be no writer. That's for fairies. *Maricones.* You want macho, you stick with me, Santiago."

Ramon looked at Harpo but didn't answer. To be macho was good. It was necessary. His father had said it again and again. Macho. Macho. Manliness. Courage. Pride.

Harpo and his gang had taunted him long enough. Taunted him, told him he should be a man, like his father, should get smart, should join them. There was a lot of money for the taking. All it needed was macho.

Ramon was as skinny as a marionette, all bony knees and elbows, and not tall enough. But it didn't take muscles to be macho, no. It took something else; something inside. OK! *Estupendo!* He'd been, all by himself long enough. He'd be macho like the rest of the gang. But was that the same macho as his father's?

As he crouched, Ramon felt sweat pouring. It was cold, but he was sweating. Well so was Harpo! And Harpo had done this a million times, while this was his first. So he could sweat. You could be macho and sweat. Besides, he was only fourteen, so even if they caught him he'd just get sent to some kid place like Spofford and be out again in six months. But Harpo, he had to sweat because he was seventeen. He'd be gone forever. They'd shave off his bushy hair and turn his head into a bowling ball. His eyes would be holes in a bowling ball. And he wouldn't be Harpo anymore. So Harpo had something to sweat about.

There was a screech of metal against metal from below as the lobby door opened and closed. Then a sound of slow footsteps on the stairs.

"Hey, that's her, I bet," Harpo whispered. "Our man was right. He's beautiful! Dopey Luis, he ain't so dopey."

Dopey Luis delivered groceries in this neighborhood, and as he went from one apartment to another, he spotted his targets. He studied everyone carefully, staring into their purses and wallets as they paid for the groceries. And he acted as if he were very stupid.

Dopey Luis stayed in the background and gave information to the gang. And for the information, he received some of the stolen money.

The footsteps were closer now, slow step by tired step. Ramon wondered again whether the old lady would be thin or fat. Then he saw her head and shoulders coming around a turn of the stairs. She was fat. She's eating good, thought Ramon, and I ain't.

He leaped up and was about to rush forward when Harpo pulled him back.

"No, stupid!" Harpo whispered. "You're always jumping! Wait! If she screams in the hallway, we're in trouble, man!"

The woman walked slowly to her door, fumbled for her key, then leaned forward. She scratched the face of the lock with her key, searching, till the key went in. She can't see good, thought Ramon. Hey, good! She can't tell my face from the man in the moon.

The woman opened the door.

"Yes!" Harpo hissed. "Now, man!"

Harpo leaped down the eight steps in a few bounds.

Before the woman could move or call out, Harpo's hand was over her mouth. Ramon saw her eyes bulge with fear. Harpo tore her handbag from her and pushed her violently into her apartment, then slammed the door. From within the apartment, Ramon heard a muffled scream.

"Out!" Harpo called to Ramon as he raced back up the stairs to the half-open window at the landing. Harpo yanked the window all the way up, climbed out to the fire escape, and raced down to the alley-way, with Ramon a few steps behind him.

"Run, you mother!" Harpo called to Ramon. "We meet where we said! Run, man!"

Ramon ran through the streets toward an empty lot near the Hudson River. He knew he should be thinking about the money, but all he could see were the woman's bulging eyes, her face rigid with terror.

"They'll do it to you, you give them a chance," Dopey Luis always said. "They *have* done it to you. Right? Now get yours back!"

Lady, lady, Ramon thought as he ran, I got to eat like anybody else. You eat plenty; you're fat. So shut your face up, lady, put your face away, and leave me alone!

2

Ramon hummed as he walked up Broadway, squinting in the morning sunlight. Under the arch of his left foot he could feel the cylinder of rolled-up bills he'd hidden there. It made him limp slightly as he walked, but he changed the limp into a skipping half jog. He ran across Forty-fifth Street just as a *Dont Walk* sign turned red.

Harpo had given him twenty-five dollars from the one hundred and four in the handbag, as well as two dollars in quarters.

"Why you giving me this?" Ramon had asked. "I didn't do nothing."

"Yeah, you did something, man. You got in my way," Harpo had answered. "Buy yourself some muscles and glue them on your arms. You can handle a knife, maybe, but without a knife, you couldn't kill a cockroach."

Ramon flushed again as he remembered that insult. But he knew Harpo was right; he was faster with a knife than anyone in Harpo's gang, but without it . . . He would never be without it! When you were short, when you were skinny, you practiced with a knife for hours. For days. He would never be without it. You couldn't be all alone, like he was, without a knife.

Ramon continued up Broadway, touching the knife in his pocket every so often. A girl his age brushed past him, bumping him slightly. She smiled at him apologetically, and in a whirl of her black hair and her large dark eyes, Ramon called *Hello* to her. But she kept walking. Go after her, he thought. No. I'd look like a nut. . . .

The girl stopped to watch a man playing three-card monte on top of an upturned crate. The man's hands moved quickly over three bent cards, as he shifted them back and forth. Ramon walked toward the small crowd and edged his way next to the girl.

"It's all fake, you know," he said quickly. "They got a guy planted in the crowd who makes a bet, see, and this guy in the crowd wins. Then they try to get you to bet. See? And you lose. . . ."

The girl looked at him with her round, solemn eyes. "Oh, I know that."

"Yeah, that's how it works."

"*Sí. Gracias.* . . ."

Then she slipped through the crowd and was gone.

Wait, wait! I want to talk to you. . . .

The crowd pressed closer to the man with the cards, as he started a new game. Ramon wondered if he should try to follow the girl again. . . . Maybe . . . No, he decided. She didn't want to talk to him or she would have hung around. . . . OK! If he wasn't good enough to talk with, then he didn't want to talk to her either!

"Keep your eye on the queen of hearts," the man with the cards called. "The queen ain't mean. Watch the queen. Ten dollars says you can't pick her. Watch the queen go home!"

It's all fake, thought Ramon. They're out hustling people at ten in the morning. A little sun and out they come. That guy there selling perfume. Stole it right off a truck. Everything's a hustle. Even them blind guys begging, they can see better than me. Hustlers, that's what they are. Yeah. . . . Hey, I'm gonna get me a hustle. 'Cause I can hustle as good as them. And when I get rich, I'm gonna have a car like I seen where they drink champagne in the backseat, and a stereo . . . and a girl like that girl, with eyes like—like big chocolate-covered almonds!

A man had slipped next to Ramon, pressing close to him. "Hey kid, what are you doing?" he asked.

He was well dressed. Suit and tie. Slightly balding. Could he be a cop, Ramon wondered. Plain clothes? But how could the guy know he had that stolen money in his shoe?

"Who me? I ain't doing nothing," Ramon answered, trying to look innocent.

"You're a . . . you're a nice kid. Want to be friends?" the man asked, nervously.

It happened often when Ramon walked along Broadway or on Forty-second Street, and it always made him angry. Why me, he thought. Why me? What do I look like?

He took a deep breath. I'm gonna get you this time. You guys with your *Do you wanna be friends . . .*

"Uh . . . what do you mean: friends?" Ramon asked.

"Friends, friends. You know . . . *friends!*"

"Oh, friends," said Ramon. "Thirty bucks."

"That's too much," said the man.

"You're crazy. Kids my age get fifty."

"Well . . . I like you. OK. Thirty. I've got a room . . . hotel." The man started walking as if he expected Ramon to follow him, but Ramon stood still. The man walked back.

"Hey kid, come on. Let's go!"

"Where's my thirty bucks?" asked Ramon.

"Where in the hell have you been, kid! That's not the way it works. I'll pay you after."

"Now."

"No." The man looked around, as if he were worried that someone could hear him.

"Half now," said Ramon.

The man looked around again. "I can't give you money on the street."

"Half now. If you don't, when you walk away,

I'll tell a cop what you're doing and you won't see daylight for a long time, man."

"You're real cute, aren't you?" The man's eyes showed edges of anger.

"Yeah. I'm what they call in the movies, making you an offer you can't refuse."

The man reached into his pocket, took out a roll of bills, and counted out a ten and five singles. "Here. You better be worth it."

"Oh mister, you'll find out I am," said Ramon.

Ramon took the bills and followed the man for a few paces, then suddenly spun around and ran in the opposite direction, dodging in and out among the passersby.

"Come back, you little spic!" the man shouted after him.

Now I'm really glad I did it, thought Ramon. No one's gonna call *me* a spic! Oh did I hustle him. He can't call a cop 'cause they'd arrest him. They think I'm gonna sell my body, they're crazy. My body's me, man. Me! Half of me. Other half's my brain. Half 'n' half. Good way to be. This fifteen bucks, I earned! New York, you are sweet! There's money everywhere! This here's one of your good days, you big stinking garbage dump! Today is New York City day!

Ramon had made a complete reversal and was walking uptown again, on Broadway. He noticed every street peddler and what each sold: bracelets, rings, perfume, sunglasses, beaded necklaces, wallets. All off trucks, he thought. All stolen off trucks. And from warehouses. I could sell that stuff easy if I knew where to get it.

There was a sudden sharp smell of bacon in the air coming from a nearby coffee shop. Oh man, I'm hungry, thought Ramon. I ain't had no breakfast. OK, I'm rich today. I got over forty bucks. I'm gonna eat till I explode.

Ramon studied a sign in the window announcing a special breakfast for $1.89. He went in and sat at the counter. The waitress came over with a damp rag and wiped the counter in front of him, then tossed a menu toward him.

"I don't need that," said Ramon. "I know what I'm getting. That there special breakfast for a buck eighty-nine. Tomato juice, two sunny-side up, bacon, toast, hashed brown potatoes, and coffee."

"Hey look, baby boy, that ain't all on the special," said the waitress. "All you get on the special is you get two sunny-side up, bacon, toast, coffee. That's all, honey. OK?"

"What do you mean!" said Ramon. "Everybody gives you hashed brown and tomato juice. Everyplace you go."

"Then go everyplace, baby boy."

"Well I'm here, and I'm hungry. But I only got a couple of dollars." Ramon took all his quarters and laid them out on the counter. "Let's see. One

11

twenty-five, one and a half, one seventy-five, two dollars. That's all I got."

"Well I got news for you, baby boy, sweetheart. You can't even get the special for that. 'Cause there's eight percent tax, makes it two dollars and four cents; I know it by heart how much."

"Hey, come on," said Ramon in his best begging voice. "Have a heart, huh, lady. I'm hungry and this is all I got. Two bucks."

"I'm sorry, baby boy."

"Quit calling me . . . Lady, please. We're like soul brother 'n' sister, right?"

"The hell we are! You are Puerto Rican, baby boy, and I'm black. Brother, my canary!"

"They spit on both of us!" said Ramon, bitter now. "Their spit tastes the same in your face like in mine."

The waitress stood staring at Ramon. She wiped the counter with her rag again, then stopped and studied Ramon further.

"Hmm," she murmured. "Where'd you get them quarters from, anyhow? You bust into a phone box or something?"

"Naa. I got this from a friend. He saw how bad I was starving."

The waitress chuckled in spite of herself. "Man, you got some real tall tales, ain't you? . . . Who spit in your face lately, anyway?"

"I dunno. There's this guy who just tried to hustle

me on the street? Only I hustled him. And he called me a spic, that's what."

"Is that all? You are living off the top of the heap, sweetheart. Come on up my neighborhood sometime; we got names for all the rats. They're real friendly. We named the biggest one after the mayor."

"We got rats, too."

"Where's that?"

"Ninth Avenue, Forty-ninth."

"Oh? That ain't bad. Could be worse." The waitress took a microphone and called into the kitchen, "One special, two eggs up, bacon, toast, hashed browns, order sausages on the side." Then she filled a large glass with tomato juice, and poured Ramon a cup of coffee.

"Hey, uh lady, uh miss, I didn't order all that stuff—"

"I know you didn't, baby boy, but you look so thin, I'm about ready to thread you for a needle and sew up this here tear in my apron. So just eat your breakfast 'n' keep shut, baby boy soul brother."

"Thanks . . . yeah, thanks. . . ."

This is what heaven is, Ramon thought as he ate. Yeah. I'll bet that's what you get first in heaven. A big breakfast. Then a shower. Then maybe another big breakfast. And then you get to meet God. That's the way I'd do it. If I was God, I wouldn't want to meet anybody who was hungry. Because when you're hungry, you're mean.

The waitress returned and gave Ramon his check. "You eat like a vacuum cleaner. Man, where do you put it?"

Ramon looked at the check. It was for a cup of coffee. Forty cents.

"Hey . . ." Ramon didn't quite know what to say. "Thanks . . . thanks . . . Nobody's ever done nothing nice like this for me before. . . ."

"Well, you stay cute and starving like you are, and you'll get plenty of females doing for you."

Ramon looked at the check again and rubbed his finger over it.

"Hey miss . . ."

"Now what?"

Ramon took three of the dollar bills he'd gotten from the man in the street and put them under the coffee cup, then put forty cents on the counter.

"What in the—! You said you were broke! You—"

"That ain't for no bill," said Ramon. "That's your tip."

"But you—"

"I'm broke for restaurants, not people. For people, it's all different. I got a different pocket with different money for people."

The waitress pushed the dollar bills back toward Ramon. "I don't need your bread, baby boy."

"I got plenty," said Ramon. "I can make money just like that. Easy. Go ahead. Take it. This way, I'll come back for breakfast tomorrow. Same way, OK?"

The waitress hesitated. "I don't like it," she said. "I thought I'd do you a favor, that's all, but now you're making it into something crooked. . . ."

"It ain't crooked. It's just getting back at *them*," said Ramon.

"Take your money, baby boy. You're heading for big trouble, you go around cheating and hustling like this. I got rats, but I got pride. Ain't you got no pride?"

Ramon took the bills and put them in his pocket. "You know, my *mamá*'s in Westside Hospital and her bed stinks, they never come around. Like the guy who owns this place? It would never happen to him! My *mamá* she's on welfare, so she's just a hunk of meat. You're no person if you're on welfare. You're just a piece of junk. That's what they think you are: junk. *You* try and be proud when your bed stinks! *You* try and be proud when everybody treats you like a rusty old piece of junk!"

3

The plant in the woven hemp hanger had long fronds, green and airy, cascading down the sides. It was the most delicate plant in the store.

"That one," Ramon said, pointing.

"That plant is very expensive," the woman in the frothy pink dress said.

"How much?"

"Twenty dollars."

"Oh. Uh . . . How about, say, fifteen for it. OK?"

"I'm sorry," the woman said, "but we have fixed prices here." She moved toward an alarm button on her desk. Ramon knew it would bring the police.

"Oh," said Ramon. "Yeah, this is a pretty high-class place. Twenty dollars, huh? . . . Well . . . it's for my *mamá*, you know. She's in the hospital. Twenty, huh? . . . It's a pretty neat-looking plant."

"Yes, it's lovely."

"Yeah . . . My *mamá*, she could use some flowers. She's got, like, what they call a nervous breakdown. She won't eat nothing 'cause she's depressed, so they got a tube stuck in her arm to feed her, and everything. OK, here's my twenty bucks."

Ramon took off his shoe and counted out twenty dollars from the cylinder of bills.

"I'm sorry," said the lady in the pink dress, "but there's eight percent tax, which brings it to twenty-one dollars and sixty cents, total."

"Oh. OK. Here's another buck sixty. Can you wrap it up?"

"Certainly. I'll put some gift wrapping on it."

"How much is that?" asked Ramon.

"There's no charge."

Ramon took the heavy package in both arms and walked to the door, then turned. "Say lady," he said, "could you help get this door open?"

The woman began fussing with some plants, as if she hadn't heard.

"Thanks." Ramon put the plant down, opened the door and held it with his foot, then picked up the plant and worked his way out the door. "Thanks, lady," he said, still holding the door with his foot. "I hope they stick something in *your* arm soon."

At the hospital, Ramon went straight to the elevator without checking in at the desk. It was a waste of time to check in; no one seemed to care about visitors. On the seventh floor, Ramon walked past the nurses' desk to a long green corridor with rooms on both sides. He stopped at Room 718, hesitated, then walked in. He tried not to smell the odor from the toilet or notice the emaciated woman staring blankly in the bed next to his mother's. As he moved close to his mother, he saw that the tube was still attached to her arm.

"Hey, mama. How are you?" Ramon asked in Spanish.

His mother seemed to be sleeping, breathing heavily through her mouth. Ramon set the plant down on the floor, pulled up a chair, and sat near the bed. She seemed smaller in the bed, no longer his bustling mother who sang along with the radio while she prepared the dinner, or shouted from the open window down to the street to call him. She seemed more like a sister, a younger sister who needed someone to protect her.

Ramon felt the knife in his right pocket. She wouldn't want him to protect her with that. His mother hated the knife; he had learned to keep it hidden. What would his father have said about it if he were home? But he was gone. And lying there in the bed, as helpless as an infant, she was gone, too.

Ramon took a small loose-leaf notebook from his left pocket. Inside the rings of the book was a stubby pencil. He had bought the book years ago, when a teacher had suggested he write things down.

He turned the pages filled with blurred sentences to a fresh sheet and wrote:

Monday, October 1.
Hospetal room. It's always the same here. This room is always green. Like that big fish tank in Mrs. Ryan's Pet Shop. The fish don't care if it's October or anything. Nether does my mamá.

Yeah, he thought, that's it. That's why I feel spooky coming here. It's like a fish tank with all the mechanical tubes and stuff. That stuff dripping from that bottle into the tube on my *mamá*'s arm. It's like that bubbling tube in the fish tank. I ought to write that down, too. Maybe it wouldn't feel so spooky no more.

His mother stirred and gave a low moan.

"Hey *mamá* . . ." Ramon said softly, shutting the book and putting it in his pocket.

His mother turned her head slightly. "Carlos?" Carlos was his father's name.

"Hey, *soy yo*, Ramon!" he said. "It's me!"

His mother twisted in the bed, then said in Spanish, "I want to go back. Carlos, please. To Cataño. Carlos . . ."

"Hey mama, it's me," Ramon continued in Spanish. "Me, Ramon. I got you a plant."

"Plant . . . plant. No more fighting. No more," she said.

Ramon climbed onto the wide window ledge and hung the plant from the drapery rod. "Hey mama, how's this?" he asked in Spanish. "Now you have something nice to look at."

His mother sat halfway up in the bed. "Carlos! Carlos! Please! No more fighting. No more! Cataño. Carlos, please!"

She didn't seem to know or care that he was standing there. He, Ramon, not his father. All she seemed to want was to be back in Cataño, in Puerto Rico, with his father. But when they'd lived in Puerto Rico, he hadn't been born yet. It was as if her unhappiness had begun with leaving Cataño, with New York, with Ramon. Is it my fault? he thought. What did *I* do?

"Carlos, Carlos, no more fighting. . . ."

No more fighting. . . . Ramon tried not to remember. His father screaming, screaming at her in Spanish. *There's no money! No money! They have all the money! They pay me like an animal!*

His father pressing his head against the bedroom wall, tired, angry. *I want to be free. We have to be free. Puerto Rico has to be free. We have to be men, not animals. Men!*

His father singing an old Puerto Rican folk song, and Ramon joining in, singing together, their voices one voice. His father and he singing . . .

His father screaming at his mother. *If I had sons, someday we could be all right. We could have money.*

But you! Only one son! Not even a son! A skinny runt! A girl! Give me some sons! All you do is sing all day! Give me sons! I want a son, not a girl!

His father taking him to Coney Island when he was small, the roller coaster, the fun house, the giant Ferris wheel. Standing in November at Coney Island, at the edge of the ocean, he and his father, shoes off, socks off, the icy water foaming.

His father demonstrating in the street, carrying a sign: **FREE PUERTO RICO!** Crowds, police. His father, face twisted with anger, pushing a policeman away. The policeman grabbing his arms. His father pushing back, hurling the sign at the officer. His father arrested. Assaulting an officer. Three years.

His father gone almost a year now.

Ramon's hands doubled into fists as he remembered. But there was no one to strike. Not the police, not his father, no one. He had struck out blindly at his father once, when his father had discovered his notebook, had laughed at him and teased him: *Sissy! Girl! Writing foolish things in a book!* And as Ramon had struck, his father had grabbed his arms and thrown him to the floor. Ramon had gotten up and tried hitting him again, and was again thrown down. And then, unexpectedly, praise: *Maybe you can be a man yet! At least you have heart to fight! To want your honor! Maybe I have a son after all. Maybe you have macho after all. . . . Now throw away that book! That's for girls!*

21

After that, Ramon had kept his notebook hidden from everyone, deep in his pocket. Even with his father gone, he kept the book hidden in the house, as if his father might see it and shout *Sissy! Girl!* from hundreds of miles away.

At least you have heart to fight! . . . Maybe you have macho after all. . . .

Did he have macho? He hadn't stopped writing in that book. . . . Still, he *was* joining the gang. He was almost a member now! Wasn't that good enough? Wasn't that macho enough? . . . He wished his father could answer.

But he was gone. Yet, somehow, his anger was there, left behind like streaked photographs. The anger was right in the hospital room. That's why she was sick! His father's anger! . . . Or was she sick because he was gone? Even his anger had been better than this emptiness. And he wasn't always angry. . . . The songs they sang . . . the ocean . . .

Ramon tore himself from his thoughts and moved closer to the bed. He tried to touch his mother's arm, but she pulled away.

"No more needles," she said in Spanish. "Carlos, please. I want to go home."

She fell back exhausted. Then for a moment she looked at the plant hanging by the window.

"Qué bonita. Qué bonita. . . ."

"It's a present," said Ramon. "From me. From Ramon."

"Gracias. Gracias, Ramón."

Why did he feel like crying, he wondered, just because she'd said his name. It was his name, wasn't it? Why shouldn't she say it?

"Hey mama, try to eat something, OK? Next time I come, I'm gonna try to sneak some ice cream in for you, OK?"

"A plant . . . yes, very pretty . . . Carlos, please . . . Carlos . . ."

Carlos again! I hate you, he thought. I hate you! You ain't never coming home! Go back to Cataño in your head! Go to hell! I ain't got no mother, and I ain't got no father, and you can both go to hell! I don't care! I don't care!

Ramon rushed out of the room and headed for the emergency stairway instead of the elevator. At the third-floor landing, he sat on the stairs and listened for oncoming footsteps, then cried silently into his hands.

The sun was in Ramon's eyes; if he looked it would blind him. He looked. A scream of light. He shut his eyes. Behind his eyelids a yellow pinwheel spun. He rubbed his eyes to make the pinwheel grow.

"Hey, why are you walking with your eyes closed, *gallo,* you rooster, you?" asked Dopey Luis.

"'Cause I'm getting high on real cheap stuff," Ramon answered.

"What? What're you taking? Let me have some," said Luis.

"Can't. This stuff can be dangerous to your health. . . . Oh, whoo! Look at that! That's beautiful! Oh man, that's great!"

"Hey come on," said Dopey Luis. "I ain't gonna give you the name and address of nobody for you to hit, if you don't give good stuff to me."

"What do you mean! You give me a name and you get part of the loot, right? For doing nothing but looking around while you deliver the bacon and toilet paper. You can't get killed like I can."

They were walking along Columbus Avenue past the white walls and bright banners of Lincoln Center. Ramon glanced at the sun and rubbed his eyes again; the fountain in the great plaza seemed to burst with yellow diamonds.

"See that! That's it!"

"That's just a fountain squirting."

"No it ain't. You stare at the sun, see? Then you rub your eyes good. Then you look at that fountain. And you're high, man."

Dopey Luis stopped walking and stared at Ramon. "Hey *gallo*, that's real stupid. That's no high. I did that when I was a baby."

Ramon shrugged. "When I was a baby they locked me in a cellar, so I never saw the sun. I never saw the sun till I was twelve."

"You are full of shit, *gallo*. I got a stash of some good stuff. Real Colombian. You want a high? I'll sell you some good stuff."

"Naa. I'm tired of that," said Ramon. " 'Cause when they locked me up, that's all they ever gave me was Colombian gold. Yeah. Like you eat cereal with milk? They gave me shredded pot with milk, instead of shredded wheat. In the dark, every day. Twice a day. That's why I'm so skinny, see. No ice cream. No potatoes. Nothing but marijuana and milk. They called it *marimilk*. Or sometimes *milkijuana*. I ate *milkijuana* in the pitch dark for twelve years."

Dopey Luis grabbed Ramon's arm and stopped him short. "Hey look, stupid! I got enough of your bull, OK? Only thing you do in the dark is play with yourself. Now I ain't gonna give you the name of this guy to hit, 'cause you're weird. You get in trouble, you'll put me in jail. I ain't doing no business with you, *gallo*."

Ramon closed his eyes again. "Hey, Luis! I just got a vision. Hey, it's beautiful! There I am, all these spotlights on me, and the cops are listening, and I'm saying, 'Yeah, Dopey Luis. He's the guy. Set up twenty, thirty jobs this year alone. Yeah. He works for Hansen's Market. Bicycle deliveries. Good guy. But he wouldn't cut me in. Kind of tough shit for him. So—' "

A knife appeared in Dopey Luis's palm. Ramon froze.

"You talk, you mother," Dopey Luis said, "and I'll cut you up so you'll never know what you are. They'll call you Ramona, *gallo*. They'll call you *gallina*."

Ramon kicked up at Dopey Luis's hand and the knife spun to the sidewalk. Ramon held his own knife now, pointed at Dopey Luis's chest.

Ramon felt his pulse beating in his head. Lucky!

26

Lucky, he thought. One in ten I could get him with that kick. Now keep it cool, man, keep it cool. . . .

"Hey Luis, come on," said Ramon. "Didn't Harpo never tell you? I'm fast. You pull a knife on me and you're dead."

Dopey Luis was backing away slightly, ready for flight. Ramon knew he was on top now. It was time for peace.

Ramon slid the blade back into the knife handle, walked over, picked up Dopey Luis's knife, and held it out to him. "Hey, come on," he said. "Give me the name of this guy and cut the crap. There's people looking at us like this is a big fight or something. Make like we're kidding around. Give me the name, huh?"

Dopey Luis looked over his shoulder. Two or three men were staring at them hesitantly, at a distance, as if expecting the fight to continue.

"Yeah, you're right," said Dopey Luis. "Let's keep walking. Come on, *gallo*."

"Give me the name!"

"Later! Walk, man!" Dopey Luis put his hand on Ramon's shoulder and steered him around the corner to a side street.

"OK," Dopey Luis said. "Now listen. This guy is a guy must be seventy-five years old, maybe eighty. He can't even walk. He's in this wheelchair all the time, OK? But he's got money. I've seen it. And he always gives me a big tip. His name's Glasser.

Twenty-four West Eighty-fourth Street. Apartment Seven E. You listening?"

"Yeah, yeah. Glasser. Twenty-four West Eighty-fourth. Seven E."

"It'll be easy. You whip out that knife, and he'll faint. He'll have a heart attack. You ring the bell, OK? And you say that you've seen the sign in the drugstore about his paintings—oh yeah, I didn't tell you: This guy's got paintings all over the place. A million paintings. They all stink. He paints these paintings, and he's got a sign in the drugstore that says *Paintings for Sale*. You tell him you seen the sign and you wanna buy a painting."

"Hey, wait a minute," Ramon said. "What's a kid like me buying a painting for? He'll never open the door! He'll call the cops!"

"OK . . . you tell him your mother's in the hospital. It's true, right? And you're buying her a painting to cheer her up and all that shit. He's been in that hospital, himself. He told me. So you can tell him all the details, see. He'll swallow it raw."

"That's pretty smart," said Ramon.

"They don't call me Dopey Luis for nothing."

"Maybe I *will* buy a painting for my *mamá*. She got a plant and all now, but she could use a painting. Hey yeah! I'll buy one off of him."

"Steal it, shithead!"

"Naa. I wouldn't steal a painting. That ain't right. I'll take his money, then I'll pay back some for one of his paintings. Yeah, that's the way. Then I can tell my *mamá* I bought it. I don't wanna lie to her."

"*Gallo*, you're the dumbest guy I ever seen."

"That's what happens when you eat nothing but shredded grass in the dark for twelve years. With skimmed milk, not even homogenized stuff. Not even no sliced bananas. No sugar, no strawberries, nothing. It's bad. Your brain turns into rice pudding. You shake your head, your brains come out your ears in little squirts. You stand on your head and—"

"Don't you never stop? What the hell you talking about, anyway?"

"You oughta know. They don't call you Dopey Luis for nothing."

5

Ramon stood near the full-length mirror, the mirror that had been brought from Puerto Rico before he was born. It was mottled with rust spots now where the silvering had worn through, but the doves carved in the wooden frame still perched along the edges, ready to fly off.

As Ramon spun around toward the mirror, his knife moved from his pocket to the palm of his hand. "Look out!" he shouted, thrusting the knife at his reflection. Then he stabbed again at the reflected living room behind him, with its wreckage of table and chairs and the iron bed where he slept.

He called to his image in the mirror, "Hey! You're gonna get enough money so you don't have to live here no more!"

Ramon turned away, then wheeled around again,

drawing the knife from his pocket once more. "Hey! *Mira! Mira!*"

Pretty good, he thought. Fast. Very fast. Yeah, I'm gonna throw all this furniture away. All I'll keep is the mirror. For practicing with my knife. The neighbors can take the rest of this shit.

He shouted toward a wall. "Hey Mrs. Garcia! You can have it all! When my *mamá* goes to the crazy house, you and everybody can tear the place apart! I don't care! I'm gonna be gone! It's yours! Hey, Mrs. Garcia! You hear? It's yours!"

Ramon went to the kitchen and saw roaches scurrying across the table. "Hey, *cucarachas*! You can tear the place apart, too!" he shouted at the roaches. "I ain't gonna try to kill any of you, no more. There's too many of you, and not enough of me. This place is yours. Eat it up! You done with the food, eat the table! Eat the linoleum! *Sí, una comilitona!* A feast! Eat the walls! Eat the ceiling! Eat each other!" He slammed his fist down on the table, killing a roach, while others bounced off from the impact. "Go ahead! This is cockroach heaven! Nobody's gonna exterminate you no more! Go ahead!"

Ramon went to the dilapidated refrigerator and opened it. A smell of spoiled food, of decaying meat, hit him. There were roaches crawling on the inside walls.

"Oh man," Ramon said softly. "How did they get in there? I should've cleaned it out good.

Hey . . . the refrigerator's warm. . . . They shut off the power on us. There ain't no electricity nowhere."

He went to a light switch and turned it on. The room remained dim.

"No lights! You gotta have money for everything! OK, freaking New York! I'll get money! You wait and see!"

Ramon felt the knife in his pocket and rubbed the long, balanced handle. The power of the knife was always there, like a lean dog pulling against its chain.

"You wait," Ramon said once more as he shut the apartment door behind him.

Mrs. Garcia was in the hallway staring at his door. She was wearing her usual torn, gray sweater.

"Who's shouting in there?" she asked in Spanish. "I heard shouting. What's the matter, Ramon? What, what?"

"Nothing," Ramon answered, also in Spanish. "The cockroaches are playing football."

"Ah! Ah! When I was a child in Puerto Rico, no one would dare speak like that to his elders. No one! Never!"

"Yes. . . . All right. . . . I'm sorry. . . ."

"Ah . . . How is your mama? She'll be home soon."

"No she won't," said Ramon. "She's getting crazier every day. She'll never come home."

"She's not crazy, your mama. She's just tired. Tired. Too much trouble. Your father. Everything. I know. Oh, I know. . . . But until she comes home, you stay with us, Ramon."

"No, I'm all right."

"But you—"

"I'm all right. I'm all right."

"But if you need help, ring my bell—"

Ramon saw that she wouldn't budge until he accepted her offer. "All right. If I need help—"

"Ah! Anytime. Day or night, you come and ring the bell."

"All right."

"Tell your mama when you see her, we miss her. Tell her we all miss her singing in the morning. I could hear her through the walls, the beautiful singing. She should have been a singer with a band. Tell her."

Ramon stared at the tiles in the hallway. Dirty unscrubbed tiles. Yes, Mrs. Garcia was right. His mother had filled the whole house when she sang. He missed it, too.

"I'll tell her," he said softly, as he slipped past Mrs. Garcia and rushed toward the stairway.

"You're just like her, Ramon," Mrs. Garcia called after him. "Full of life. Tell her I said so. Tell her."

Just like her, thought Ramon. Then maybe I'll be going crazy soon, too. If the cops don't get me first.

He raced down the stairs and out the broken front door. Across the street two trees were turning yellow in the first October chill, a pale yellow as if they had been bleached by the pavement around them.

Ramon often stared at those thin trees from his front window, imagining they were the ghosts of trees, trees from another planet. The sad trees, his mother had called them. The poor trees. Not like in Cataño, where people were poor, but the trees and flowers were rich.

"That's what this city does to us," she had whispered to him in Spanish one night, when his father was angry. "It kills us little by little, like those trees out front. It's killing *him*," she'd said, as she'd nodded toward his father in the other room.

As Ramon crossed the street and walked toward the trees, he remembered how he'd whispered back to his mother, "Well it isn't going to kill me! I'll kill this city first!" In front of the trees he felt the same anger he'd felt that night. His father's anger inside his own chest.

Maybe his father was right about things. Maybe you had to be macho to survive. Maybe you had to be angry to survive.

Ramon touched the trees for luck, as he often did. Luck for himself and for his knife. For what was coming. He murmured again, "It ain't gonna kill me. . . ."

Then he turned and headed uptown toward the man in the wheelchair on Eighty-fourth Street.

Dopey Luis's man. Ramon walked carefully, aware of every step. He thought of taking the bus, but decided that walking was better. Walking gave him more time.

"Hey, Ramon!" a familiar voice called. It was Felipe. "Where you going? I'll walk you."

Felipe had been in Ramon's class in junior high and had graduated second in the school. Some of the boys called him Book-Eyes because of his glasses and squint. And his endless books.

Oh mama, thought Ramon. I gotta get rid of him. He's a good guy, but once he starts, he never lets go.

"Hey, Felipe. *Qué pasa?*" asked Ramon.

"*Nada,*" said Felipe. "What's happening with you? I don't see you down the high school."

"I was there all week, a week ago. But I got a lot of stuff I gotta do, you know?"

"Yeah, I know. How's your mother? I hear she's sick."

"She ain't too good."

"That's pretty tough. . . . How's your father making out?"

Ramon started to answer, then hesitated. Was Felipe setting him up to insult him? . . . No, Felipe never insulted anyone. He was just being extra polite as always. Annoyingly polite. Ramon decided to cut through all the politeness and give Felipe real answers to his questions.

"I dunno," said Ramon. "My *papá*, he don't want

me to visit him. Never. He don't want me to see him, you know, where he is. In that freaking jail."

"Yeah, it's tough," said Felipe.

"We went up there once," Ramon continued, "but he wouldn't come out to the visiting room. My *mamá*, she cried on the train all the way back. Shit! He could've come out! At least for her! Right?"

"I guess so. . . . Yeah. It's really tough," said Felipe nervously. Then he quickly changed the subject. "Hey, let's stop in that bookstore on Fifty-seventh Street a minute, OK? They got a book I want."

"Naa. I gotta go. I'll see you around," said Ramon, trying to move away from Felipe.

"OK, I'll walk you," said Felipe. "I can get that book later."

I gotta trick him out, thought Ramon. I don't want him to see where I'm going or anything.

"Naa, let's go in the bookstore," said Ramon. "What kind of book are you getting?"

"*Gray's Anatomy*. Doctors have been using that book for like fifty years. And now people can get it for only six bucks."

"Hey Felipe, you still gonna be a shrink?"

"Neurologist. That's different than a shrink."

"Oh yeah? Hey, that's good! I can't even spell it!"

Anatomy books, thought Ramon. Neurologist. He's really smart, but no wonder they call him Felipe-the-Weirdo and Book-Eyes and all. That's what they'd start calling me, if I let them. . . .

While Felipe studied the heavy anatomy book, Ramon browsed among the large gift books on display, watching Felipe at a distance. He flipped through a book on the art of Norman Rockwell, another on Picasso's early paintings, and huge books on French cooking, Hollywood horror movies, and pinup girls of the past. He thought of buying his mother the pinup book as a joke, then keeping it for himself.

Ramon looked down the aisles filled with books. All those writers. Could it ever happen to him? Could he ever write a book? A book about Puerto Rico, maybe. . . . Would his father call him a girl or sissy then! . . . No, it was impossible. All he could do was write junk in a shitty notebook.

Felipe was at the front register paying for his book. Ramon rushed over, nudged Felipe, and said, "Hey Felipe, I gotta get going. I'll see you around, OK?"

"Hey wait!" called Felipe as he handed the money to the cashier.

But Ramon was out of the store and racing down the block. Oh mama, I hate to dump him like that, thought Ramon. He's, like, a friend. But I got business to do. Besides, anybody in the gang sees me with him, they'll think I'm getting weird too. Book-Eyes, he's on his own. I got enough problems.

6

Ramon studied the names next to the buttons in the outer lobby of the gray-brick apartment house. 5A Carlino, 5B Samuelson, 5C Deitz, 5D Rosen, 5E Morrison, 5F Friedenthal. Then his eyes jumped: 7D Costanza, 7E Glasser.

Glasser. Rich. Rich and living on top of the world, with air conditioning and a carpet in the lobby. Hey Glasser, he thought, I hate your freaking guts. I'm gonna take care of you, Glasser.

Ramon pressed the button for Morrison and waited. When the buzzer for the lobby door didn't signal, he pressed the button for Deitz. The buzzer sounded and Ramon pushed the door open.

The lobby smelled of old carpeting and cleaning fluid. Ramon walked into the open elevator and pushed the button for the seventh floor. The heavy door slid closed with a smooth hum and the elevator whirred upward.

Ramon's hands felt cold. He touched the knife in his pocket. Glasser, I hate you, he thought. I only rip off people I hate, and I hate you.

The elevator door hummed open. Ramon walked to the left. 7H . . . 7J . . . 7K . . . Wrong way, he thought. Why did his hands feel so cold?

He walked to the right. 7G . . . 7F . . . 7E. OK. Now. He pressed the buzzer. Glasser, I hate you. He pressed again.

"Who?" came a voice from behind the door.

Act, he thought. Like you're in a play! Act! It's like a school play, that's all!

"Uh . . . It's me. . . . I saw that sign in the drugstore, you know . . . and I want to buy a painting, like, for my *mamá*."

"Show your face. I can't see you," said the voice.

Ramon stood in front of the round viewing port in the door and smiled. Act! Act!

"Yeah, my *mamá*'s sick over in Westside Hospital. And I thought maybe I'll buy her a painting. You know, to cheer her up."

"How old are you?" asked the man behind the door.

"Me? I was fourteen last month."

Ramon heard a metallic rasping and a series of clicks. The door opened. An elderly man in a brown sweater was holding on to the door. His hair was white and wild, and he had a two-days' growth of gray beard. The man slumped back down into a wheelchair behind him.

"You know," he said, "if you were a day older than fourteen and a month, I wouldn't let you in. . . . Say, you don't look like you can afford a peanut-butter sandwich, let alone a painting—"

The knife was in Ramon's hand, aimed at Glasser's chest. Ramon felt strangely removed from himself, as if he truly were only acting. What should he say to the man?

"I want . . . I want all your money, Glasser."

"You know my name?"

"Yeah."

"That's beautiful! . . . All right, go ahead! Use your knife! You little punk hoodlum! Go ahead, use it!"

He's just bluffing, thought Ramon. Trying to trick me out.

"I only want money," he forced himself to say calmly.

Glasser started wheeling backward into the living room, steering his wheelchair skillfully, turning it sharply to the left and right.

"I'm not going to give you any money, you two-bit bum. You've got a knife. I'm a cripple. What more do you need? Kill me! Go ahead! Then you can take everything. Money. Paintings. My underwear. Who cares? Do it already!"

This ain't just a trick, thought Ramon. This guy's nuts. He's messing me up. What do I do? . . . Let's see what he's got worth taking. . . .

Ramon looked around the room, but there was nothing worth stealing; only books and paintings. There were paintings everywhere: on the walls, leaning against bookcases, piled on chairs. In a quick glance he saw faces, trees, city streets in bright yellows, reds, blues, greens. They glowed like the fish he'd seen once in the aquarium at Coney Island. Had seen with his father. His father who could be as gentle as the gliding fish. But then: *Give me sons! I want a son, not a girl!* . . . OK! Is this macho enough for you? Ramon shouted in his mind. Is it!

"What are you waiting for, you bum!" Glasser called to him. "Do it!"

"Hey, I just want, like, your money and—"

"Oh, you'll get my money. Twelve dollars, that's my money. You'll be a big shot. Man found knifed; murdered for twelve dollars. Paintings stolen. Yes, take all the paintings. Clear out all that garbage! And stick that knife in me. Then they can clear the rest of the garbage out: *me!* You hear! The rest of the garbage!"

He was crazy! He was! Dopey Luis had given him a crazy guy.

"Kill me! End it for me already, you stupid, mindless, dumb animal! Like an earthquake! Like a fire! End it!" Glasser swung his wheelchair around, purposely blocking Ramon's way to the door, as if to force Ramon to act.

Ramon felt trapped. He couldn't think. If Harpo were with him, what would Harpo do? . . . Cool it. Cool it, that's what. Before he gets all the neighbors in here with his yelling. Talk nice to the man. Talk nice.

"I . . . I only want money . . . and a painting. . . . I . . . I want a painting. I like them. Yeah."

"*You* like them! *You!* Then they *must* be garbage!"

"I like them. I'm gonna give one to my *mamá*—"

"His mama! He stands with a knife, this terrorist, this murderer, and he's going to give a painting to his mama! You're a lunatic!"

"Me? You're a lunatic, not me! You act like you want me to kill you!"

"I do. I've had enough. Enough of this world. More than enough. Do you understand that! So kill me and be finished!"

"No. I won't kill nobody—"

"Then put that knife away!" Glasser said. "When I hold a paintbrush I paint, garbage or not! If you're holding a knife, use it! You want money, take it! You want one of these paintings? You want my garbage? Take it, too! You punk!"

Cool it. . . . Talk nice to the man. . . .

"They . . . they ain't garbage—"

"Yes, garbage!"

Talk nice, talk nice. Keep talking. . . .

"That one there." Ramon pointed with his knife at a bright yellow-and-red painting. "And over there. That's good stuff. Yeah. You know what that stuff looks like? Like them kites in Central Park. You know? Like you look at the sky and there's something there you don't expect. The sky is all full of surprises. And that's what your paintings are, they're all—"

"Say that again!" Glasser leaned forward in his wheelchair.

"Huh?"

"What you just said."

"I don't know what I said."

"The sky is . . ."

"Oh. You mean, like, the sky is full of surprises? Them kites?"

"Yes, *them* kites." With a quick movement, Glasser pulled a cigarette from a pack in his sweater pocket and lit it with a flick of his thumb on a match. He inhaled deeply and blew the smoke out toward the ceiling.

"Since you're not going to kill me yet," Glasser continued, "I'll tell you something. What you just said is as good as any of those paintings. Better! Do you understand?"

"No . . . I don't know. . . ." Was this another trick? Ramon wondered. Or was Glasser just being crazy all over the place.

"Of course you don't know. Because you're stupid, even though you're obviously not stupid. So here's

43

my advice, punk. Take the money. It's on the kitchen table. Take it. Keep robbing. Keep holding that knife. Buy a couple of guns. Use the guns. Be a big man with the knives and the guns. Kill or be killed. It's a living. Till you die. Good! Go! Good-bye! Who am I to tell you what to do. The sky is full of surprises? Worthless. Just like these paintings. Take the money and run. Keep running. With the sky full of surprises, you could end up like me. With a living room full of surprises and a kitchen full of ants. So take the money and get the hell out of here, since you're not in a killing mood today, punk!"

Glasser wheeled out of Ramon's path, then held his hand out toward the kitchen as if welcoming Ramon to the money. Ramon hesitated, looking around the room once more, then back at Glasser.

There was no use trying to figure it out. Ramon walked backward to the kitchen, still watching Glasser, then rushed over to the table and scooped up the bills.

With the money jammed into his pocket, Ramon rushed to the door and down the emergency stairway out to the street.

What was so big about kites and surprises? Ramon wondered. It didn't really matter. Because anybody could see that Glasser was crazy. Even though he could really paint good.

7

They were all there. Harpo, Dopey Luis, Angel, Julio, the whole gang. The gang with the secret name, a name Ramon still hadn't learned. They prided themselves on having no special jackets, no name emblazoned on their backs to be seen by everyone. The police could never say that the Green Lions or the Flames had robbed someone. Other gangs sometimes called them Harpo's Gang, but it wasn't their name.

This is it, thought Ramon. I bet they're gonna make me a member 'cause I've done a job. They're gonna tell me the name, and everything. Harpo, he ordered me to come to their meeting, so I'm in!

The meeting place was on the third floor of an abandoned building near the Hudson River docks. Chunks of plaster and strips of lath covered the floor, and the smell of rotting garbage was everywhere. As they sat leaning against the bare walls waiting for Harpo to begin, Ramon noticed Angel poised with a chunk of plaster in his raised hand. A rat streaked past the door and Angel hurled the plaster at it. The plaster exploded into gray shrapnel against a handrail in the hall.

"Shit!" shouted Harpo. "Quit throwing that plaster out the door, Angel!"

"I wanna get a rat—"

"Hey! We got, what do you call it, we got a big-game hunter here! Angel the Rat Killer! That's a good name. Let's use it from now on. Angel the Rat Killer."

"No!" shouted Angel.

"Then leave that plaster alone, and shut up and listen, OK? . . . I said shut up! . . . OK. Let's start. First thing we gotta talk about is this freak, Ramon Santiago, here, who grabs maybe two hundred dollars, maybe three hundred, and says he got twelve. Twelve dollars! You heard me! Twelve freaking bucks! If it wasn't because of your father, you little shit, I'd break your ass for you. I swear I would. But since your father beat up a freaking cop—"

"That's all there was!" Ramon shouted. "This guy Glasser got no money!"

"You lying little bastard! You skinny little— Man, I took you with me! I showed you how! I let you in! *Bastardo!*"

"No! There was no money! He said that's all he

had!" Ramon tried to think. Don't pull your knife! There's too many!

"Listen to that!" Harpo jeered. "He told him that's all he had. Hey, don't look around, kid, 'cause that's all I got. . . . OK, thank you, mister. I'll take the twelve. Good night. . . . You stupid faggot! You dumb freak! You think I'm crazy! You think I believe anybody could be that dumb! You asked *permission* to rip this guy off! Who believes it! Who? You, Angel? Luis? Julio? Who believes it?"

There was a long silence. Then Julio said softly, "Ahh, I dunno. I believe him. It ain't worth two hundred dollars to nobody to make up a story and look that dumb. Ramon, he's too freaking young for us, that's all. He's a freaking baby."

"I ain't too young!" said Ramon. "This guy is really poor! I ain't dumb. And I ain't too young. The guy is just poor!"

"Hey, *gallo,* now you're calling *me* dumb," said Dopey Luis. "I seen at least eight twenty-dollar bills in that guy's wallet. I seen it! You think I'd send anybody out for a freaking twelve bucks!"

"Well he ain't got it no more," said Ramon. "Maybe he spent it on grocery stuff. Or shoes. Or paint. He paints. He paints good!"

"Who cares, man! He's got the money!" said Dopey Luis. "The guy lives in a good building. They got air conditioning in the place. An elevator. Everything. He's freaking rich!"

Ramon's mind raced in and out of each argument,

like a rabbit searching for a hole. "Listen, listen! On welfare they sometimes give you good apartments, even a TV. I know. My *mamá*, she got TV, even though she's on welfare."

"How about air conditioning, *gallo*!"

"She never asked for it. She never asked for nothing. I'm proud, I'm proud. That's all she ever says. And now she's going crazy, in a hospital, and she doesn't even know who I am, and I wouldn't lie to you, 'cause I wanna be in your gang, and I wouldn't lie! He didn't have no money. He didn't! Here! Take the money that's left from the last time. I don't want it. I don't need it. Here!" Ramon pulled off his shoe and threw the roll of bills onto the floor.

There was silence again, as Harpo scratched his head. Then, abruptly, Harpo kicked the roll of bills back toward Ramon.

"OK, baby, take your money," said Harpo. "Julio's right, baby. I believe you! All you took is twelve bucks! Now you better believe me! This guy's got two or three hundred more. If Luis says he's got it, he's got it."

Maybe Glasser did have it, thought Ramon, as he put the money back in his shoe. It was dumb to listen to Glasser. *Twelve dollars. It's on the kitchen table.* He hadn't checked Glasser's wallet. Or the shelves in the living room. Nothing. They were right; he was stupid.

"OK, listen," said Ramon. "I'll go back. OK? I'll get the rest. OK?"

"Sure," said Dopey Luis. "You just knock on the door and say, 'Hey Glasser, sweetheart, let me in please. I'm the little bastard that stole your twelve bucks and now I want the rest. Nice to see you again!' "

"I can get in, don't worry," said Ramon.

"How?" asked Harpo.

"I got a way."

"What way? How, man?"

"Let me do it! I'll do it, don't worry. Nobody's gonna make *me* look stupid," said Ramon.

"You get caught, man, you don't know who we are," said Harpo. "Don't forget it!"

"Yeah, I know!"

"Then get the hell out of here!" said Harpo. "Go play with that faggot weirdo I seen you with, Felipe Book-Eyes. We have stuff here we have to talk about."

Ramon hesitated, then said, "Felipe's OK." Saying that to Harpo had to be plain dumb. Why did he say it! To be macho? What kind of macho was that? The dumb kind.

"Oh yeah?" said Harpo. "Then let *Felipe* get that money! Come on, man, beat it!"

"If I take the money," said Ramon, "if I can go back in there and take two, three hundred, do I get into the gang?"

49

"Get into the gang? You kidding! Man, if you can get that money anymore, I personally will kiss your rear end. In front of everybody. OK? Now get the hell out of here!"

Ramon went down the shaky stairway to the lobby strewn with newspapers and burst garbage bags. I'll get that money all right, he thought. I'll figure something out. I just gotta crank up my brain, that's all.

He walked slowly along Eleventh Avenue toward Fifty-third Street, toward his special spot, his thinking place. Far below street level, in a deep gully, were the weed-covered tracks of an abandoned railroad line. Dozens of worn-out truck and auto tires lay along the tracks, rolled down the embankment by men who worked in the nearby auto-repair shops. Hulks of old refrigerators, boilers, twisted parts of shattered cars, all had been heaved down into the gully, now used as a dumping ground.

Ramon slipped through a break in the chain link fence and scrambled down the embankment to the tracks. From below, the street above him couldn't be seen. He sat in a spot he knew well, where scraggly bushes and high weeds hid much of the debris.

He lay back and looked up at the sky, narrowing his eyes until he could see only the tops of the weeds; no buildings, no tires, no twisted car fenders, only clouds and weeds. He started to daydream. It was a continuing story that he returned to each time he lay in the railroad cut.

In the story he was another boy in another place, in Indiana or Illinois, some place he had never been. A boy with a father who drove to work every morning like fathers on TV, with a mother who cooked dinners in a kitchen with light through big windows, light brighter than the light in this gully.

He let himself become that other boy, a boy who had gone down to the railroad tracks behind his small town to meet his friends and fish in the nearby pond. And he changed his name from Ramon to Peter. No, to Lance. This time it would be Lance. And all afternoon he and his friends fished among weeds at the edge of the pond.

Then he saw himself going home for dinner to a white frame house, a two-story house with bushes and trees in front. To have supper with his Mom and Dad and his older brother, Ken, and his younger sister, Diane, whom he always teased but always helped when she had problems, like older brothers on TV.

And there's this dance, he thought, like, we're all going to the dance together, me and Kenny and Diane. And the school gym is full of balloons and ribbons and crepe-paper decorations, and my shoes hurt because they're new, so I take off my shoes, hey yeah, I'm gonna dance in my socks, no wait, I'll take off my socks too, and that girl, she's laughing at me, but like friendly, and she takes off her shoes, too, and we're starting to dance and—

EEE-AWW! EEE-AWW! Sirens. Police sirens

woke him as always. EEE-AWW! EEE-AWW! Like giant donkeys braying, howling, laughing at him. At him, Ramon, with his torn jacket, lying amid scrub grass, with money in his shoe, and a knife in his pocket pressing against his thigh.

The hulks of dead refrigerators came back into focus. The tires, great black zeros, yawned at him in the sunlight.

Yeah, he thought, I better think about that guy, Glasser. I don't wanna think about him, but I have to. . . . In a minute. I will, in a minute.

Ramon took out the wire-bound book from his left pocket, touching his right pocket quickly to make sure the knife was still there. He turned the pages to a clean sheet, sat up straight in the weeds and wrote:

Wednesday, October 3.
Angel. If Angel keeps throwing stuff at rats, he's going to become a rat-angel. I want to join the gang, but I hate his angel guts.

Ramon reread what he'd written. That feels good, he thought. Now I don't even hate that freak as much. He continued to write:

Tires. All alone, tires look like wird . . . weird spaceships landed from Mars. And I'm as weird as the tires, writing this stuff down. . . . Glasser. Glasser paints what's in his head like I'm writing now. That's why he's crazy and so am I. I got his crazy twelve dollers and—

Ramon looked up and whistled. He'd had a sudden idea. Hey, maybe . . . Yeah! That could work, he thought. Now I know how to get back into Glasser's apartment. The twelve-dollar caper, that's what I'll call it. I'm gonna try it! First thing tomorrow!

Ramon slipped the twelve dollars he'd stolen under the door of Glasser's apartment. Then he quickly wrote a note on a page of his book, tore out the sheet, and pushed it under the door. The note read: *The sky is full of suprises, and here's one more suprise. Yours truly, punk.* He paused a moment, then rang the bell.

Ramon put his ear to the door and heard the wheelchair coming down the foyer. There was a long pause. He must be reading the note, thought Ramon. He counted to five, then rang the bell again.

"Yes! Yes!" called Glasser. "I'm here; I'm here! What do you want? Forgiveness? Cheap and plenty? You're forgiven, punk! Now go home!"

"I wanna buy a painting, for real," called Ramon. "I wanna buy that blue-and-green one you got over the table. Where you painted a lady in a blue dress, only it's all blurred? And there's this bowl of apples and all the apples are green? That one. OK? For my *mamá* in the hospital."

"You remember all that! You're a punk with a good memory, punk!" Glasser called through the door.

"And that lady in the picture, she's holding one of the apples and her hand is, like, almost transparent. So you can see the apple right through her fingers. I remember everything. It's my favorite. . . ."

"Good! If you like it so much, you can have it. A gift. From my vast collection. See! You don't need a knife, punk!"

There was a clicking of door locks. And Harpo said he'd never get back in. It had been so easy. Glasser was really *estúpido*. An idiot!

The door opened. Glasser, still wearing his old brown sweater, waved Ramon toward the living room. Ramon hesitated.

"Come in, come in. Get your painting," said Glasser.

Ramon walked past the kitchen while Glasser followed in his wheelchair. In the living room Ramon looked around nervously, wondering where he should start searching for money.

"The painting's over there," said Glasser, pointing toward a wall.

"Yeah, I know," said Ramon. "Uh . . . I wanna look around first, OK?"

"Look all you want. You can have any painting

55

you like. I'm very bighearted with my masterpieces."

"What's behind this stuff?" asked Ramon, pushing aside some books on a shelf.

"I thought you wanted a painting. Now what do you want? A book? Take a book. Some fruit? Take an apple. Be my guest!"

"All I want is money," said Ramon. His voice felt strange and bodiless, as if it were echoing in an empty room. "I hear like you were lying. I hear you got a lot of money hidden someplace."

Glasser slumped back in his wheelchair. "So . . ." he said quietly. "So . . . money again, is it? Well, well. Glasser, the *schlemiel*, loses another bet on the human beast. Some surprises your sky is full of! . . . All right! Tear the place apart, my friend! Bash the walls in! Maybe you'll find the secret of existence. In the meantime, I'm continuing my painting. As they say in the street, up yours, you lousy punk!"

Glasser wheeled his chair around, took a paintbrush, and started working on an unfinished painting.

"Punk!" he shouted.

"Liar!" Ramon shouted back. "You got money! You lied last time!"

"Then find it! I have millions! Find it, bum! Lying about your own mother being sick! And you call *me* a liar! Bum!" Glasser angrily slashed his brush across the canvas.

"*Bastardo!* She is sick!" Ramon hurled himself at a bookcase, tearing into the books like a lion into meat. Books flew everywhere as he pulled the volumes from shelf after shelf.

Glasser, without turning, continued to paint, one angry stroke after another.

"Fourteen years old! This is America today! Fourteen years old and *look*!" he shouted as he painted.

"Where's the money, you liar! Where?"

"I swallowed it! You'll have to cut me open! Time for your knife again!"

"You're a liar! You're rich! You got air conditioning! You're rich!"

Ramon hurled paintings aside, tore clothing from a closet, even pulled up the carpet.

"Give me your wallet!" he shouted at Glasser. Glasser took out his wallet and threw it at Ramon's feet.

"Pick it up, bum!"

Ramon shook the wallet open and pulled out the twelve dollars. He hurled the money and wallet onto the floor. Where was the real money? The bedroom! Maybe the bedroom! But Glasser could phone the police while he was out of the living room. He'd have to cut the phone cord with his knife.

"Hey!" he called. "Where's your phone?"

"What phone? Who calls me?"

Ramon went into the bedroom and started pulling the blanket off the bed. It's here, it's here, he thought. Somewhere! It's got to be here! He yanked the drawers out of a bureau and dumped underwear, pajamas, and socks over the floor. Then he rushed back to the living room. Glasser was still painting.

Ramon kicked the books on the floor aside, trying to find something, anything that looked valuable. He knelt amid a jumble of paintings and books, clawing through them, searching for something he could take back, something to prove to Harpo and Angel and Dopey Luis that he'd done his best. That he wasn't lying to them. There was nothing there! Nothing! All the man had were books, paintings, and junk!

Ramon sat panting and sweating in the middle of all the rubble, feeling dazed and shaky, the way he felt after running a long distance. Dopey Luis was wrong! Glasser was poor. He didn't have anything.

"Finished?" asked Glasser, still painting.

"No!" said Ramon. "Tell me where you hid the money. You're rich! Where's your money! *Tell me!*"

"Look in the refrigerator," said Glasser quietly. "That's where the whole story of my life is. Money. Fame. Fortune. Go ahead. Look."

Ramon rushed to the kitchen and pulled open the refrigerator door. He saw a chunk of old cheese on the top rack. Two apples. Some bread. A milk container with a lip of curdled milk. A banana, overripe and black. Other bits of food. It was just like his own refrigerator at home.

Glasser was poor. He had to be. Nobody with any money would live like that. Ramon walked back to the living room, feeling ugly, inside and out. The man was as poor as he was. Maybe poorer, because he couldn't hustle at all anymore. He was too old.

"They said you had money," Ramon mumbled. "Hidden, you know. . . . I . . . you know . . . I'm sorry. . . .

"He's sorry! This criminal hoodlum tears my apartment to shreds, *but!* BUT! He's sorry! Western civilization triumphs again!"

"They, you know, they said . . . Anyway, they were wrong—"

"Who is this *they*?"

"I . . . I gotta go," said Ramon nervously.

"Naturally. I understand. You have another social engagement. What is it, a murder downtown? A kidnaping on the East Side? Look at my apartment, look! Why the hell don't you at least fix it up if you're so sorry! Hah!"

"Yeah. I . . . I'll put the books back."

"The books? How about putting everything back! You're sorry? Then do something, bum!"

"I'll put them back . . . but you quit calling me bum," said Ramon.

"What should I call you then, juvenile delinquent? Do you like that better?"

"No!" Ramon shouted. Couldn't the man see he was sorry!

"All right! What do you think I should call you? *You* tell *me*!"

"Ramon . . ."

Glasser studied Ramon for a moment, then nodded his head, slowly. "All right," he said. "All right. Another bet; my last. Believe me, it's my last. Ready? Here goes. . . . Please—notice the *please*!—pick up my clothing and paintings and books . . . *Ramon*. Then take the painting you liked, just as before, as if nothing had happened, take it as a gift and give it to your mother, who—I believe you—is sick. Take it as a gift from me to you . . . Ramon. How's *that* for a betting man?"

He's crazy, thought Ramon. I try to rob him twice, and he's giving me a painting. He's gotta be crazy. I wouldn't give nobody a painting after this! Nobody!

"Hey . . . thanks . . . thanks . . ." Ramon mumbled.

"Yes, you're welcome. . . . You think I'm a lunatic, don't you; I can tell from your face. Well I am; so what!"

Ramon flushed. Glasser seemed to be reading his mind.

"I don't think you're no lunatic," Ramon said quickly, as he started clearing up the room.

"That's a double negative! That means you think I *am* a lunatic. Which I am. Do you know what a double negative is?"

"No."

"*I don't think you're no lunatic* is a double negative. You should say 'I don't think you're a lunatic.' But you can't say that because I *am* a lunatic. Therefore, you should say 'You are not no lunatic' which would be correct in this case. Do you understand?"

Ramon tried to keep from smiling. Was Glasser really crazy, or was he just laughing at himself and Ramon at the same time?

"Do you understand? I'm asking!"

"No, I don't understand nothing that you said about not being no lunatic!" Ramon stared directly at Glasser with the edge of a smirk showing.

"A wise guy, hey! There's a brain somewhere behind all the punk baloney, hey?"

"Naa . . . I ain't got no brain nowhere."

"Very good, punk . . . I mean, Ramon. Very good."

"*Muchas gracias, Señor Loco* . . . I mean Glasser," said Ramon, the smirk spreading.

"*Señor Loco*, hey? Mister Lunatic . . . I like that. That's me! *Señor Loco*. Beautiful!"

He's crazy, all right, thought Ramon. Any man that likes to be called crazy, he's got to be crazy. Maybe that's what he could tell Harpo and the others. He'd have to tell them something! Glasser was crazy so he gave all his money away. The same way he'd given this painting to him. Would they believe that? Because they'd never believe he was just poor, even though it was the truth.

9

Ramon looked at the books as he put them back on the shelves. He'd never heard of any of them. *The Philosophy of Spinoza. The Brothers Karamazov. The Magic Mountain* . . . that one sounded interesting, but it was too thick. . . . *German Expressionist Painting. Le Père Goriot.* Books. Endless books. Books full of paintings. Books of photographs. Of poetry. Books in German. In French. Books without covers, held together by rubber bands. Ramon wondered if all these writers had started by writing things down in a notebook as he did.

"Hey, you read a lot of stuff," said Ramon, flipping through the pages of a thick magazine.

"Not anymore," said Glasser. "I spit on all that. This world stinks, my friend, and books make no difference. None!"

"Naa. I don't agree."

"He doesn't agree! Read a book first, then you can disagree!"

"Yeah. Anyway, you got millions of books," Ramon said, deciding not to answer Glasser's insults. "Hey, Glasser. How come you got all these books, and, like, you got air conditioning and a carpet in the lobby? But you got nothing in your refrigerator."

"I'm on welfare, idiot!"

"Yeah, so are we. But we don't have a carpet or anything. You oughta see our lobby door. They put in wood, you know, 'cause the glass got busted. Now the wood panel's busted, too. We just got air there. Our lobby door is half made of air."

"Hmm . . . I like that," Glasser said almost to himself. "A door half made of air. You're a natural poet, you stupid moron."

"Yeah, that's what one of my teachers said. But he was full of shit. . . . Anyway, how come you got nothing to eat? Even *we* got more."

"I'd rather spend the money on paint. Once or twice a month I buy food for two weeks. Then I buy paint with the rest. See?"

"Yeah. . . ." So that's why Dopey Luis figured he was rich, thought Ramon. A lot of groceries, once in a while. And all the rest for paint. Would Harpo believe that? No. None of them would.

"All right," said Glasser. "Now would you mind getting back to work. This room is still a mess."

"I'm done, except for the paintings."

"The paintings? You don't have to put them back. Just kick them in a corner where they belong. Wait! Better yet! Throw them all out. Thank you."

He's crazy again, thought Ramon. OK, let's see what he does. "Hey Glasser," he said. "Which ones do I throw out first?"

"All of them! Or give them to your mother. She can open a gift shop and sell them cut rate."

"Yeah, OK. I'll give them . . . I'll . . . Hey . . . hey wait a minute . . . I got an idea!"

What an idea, he thought. Could it work? With these paintings? . . . Sure! Why not! My hustle! This could be my hustle! Yeah! I can sell this guy's paintings!

"Hey Glasser!"

"What now?"

"If I could sell your paintings, like, how much would you give me?"

"Sell them! You? Are you crazy?"

"No, I mean it. I can sell them."

"How are you going to sell them, if I can't? Nobody wants my work anymore. You know what a has-been is? Me, that's what!"

"Don't worry. I'll hustle them. I'll sell them with some jive, man."

"Jive? What jive?"

"I'll figure something out. We'll split fifty-fifty, OK? Is it a deal?"

"How can I stop you? You could knock me out

64

with a baseball bat and take everything, anyway."

"OK, then it's a deal," said Ramon with finality.

"A robber *and* a businessman. Excellent combination. You will go far."

"Thanks. How much you think I should get for a painting?"

"Ten cents."

"Come on, Glasser!"

"Fifty cents. At most, a dollar."

"Then what's the use of painting?" asked Ramon. "The paint costs more than that, right? Why paint, man?"

"I paint to get things out of my system, not for money," said Glasser.

"Huh? I don't get it."

Glasser scratched his face and stared at Ramon, as if trying to decide whether to continue. He pulled out his cigarettes.

"I don't know why I'm bothering to explain this to you, but . . ." Glasser gestured toward a painting lying on the floor. "Look over there. See that yellow-and-gold painting? You think it's just a lot of autumn leaves? Well you wouldn't know it, but that's me, laughing. And that one of the blue-and-gray house? With only one light on? That's me, too. Crying, I suppose. I painted that one years ago, just after my wife died. It made me feel better to paint it; to get it out. That's all. I paint to feel better. Or to feel, period."

Ramon nodded. It was exactly how he'd felt down

in the gully, writing about Angel. And in the hospital room. He wondered if he should tell Glasser about his notebook. But the things he wrote were stupid, not like these multicolored paintings, clear and bright as new marbles. He rubbed his finger across the painting of the house.

"Hey, that's good," he said. "That's too good to sell."

"Well, maybe I'll keep that one," said Glasser. "But the rest, sell them, burn them. Who cares. Do whatever you like."

"OK! It's too late today, but tomorrow I'm gonna sell them all! I'll start with maybe five, OK?" Ramon was close to dancing. He knew he could sell the paintings; they were magnificent.

"Take what you want," said Glasser. "Good-bye and good riddance."

"OK. That one," said Ramon, pointing. "And, uh, that one. And let me see . . . that one there. . . . And can I still have the one you said you'd give me? For myself?" Ramon gestured toward the painting of the woman in blue, holding an apple.

Glasser wheeled over to the painting, took it off the wall, and handed it to Ramon. "It's yours," he said. "I always paint a painting for *someone*. Even for muggers. This one must have been for you. Who can tell."

"Hey, thanks. I'll hang it up in my house, OK?"

Ramon collected the unframed canvases and stacked them under his arm. "Hey, I can carry all of them. They fit good," he said as he moved toward the door. "I'll be back tomorrow with your dough. Fifty-fifty. Then I'll get the next bunch of paintings."

"You'll be back? I'll bet. If you don't mind, I won't hold my breath."

"Naa. I don't mind. But I'll be back. So long, Glasser."

Ramon slipped out the door, tightening his grip on the paintings. In the elevator, he studied the canvases stretched taut as drumheads over the wooden frames. As he rubbed his fingers over the thick paint, he could feel the froth of waves, the bricks of an orange building, the smooth skin of the woman with the bowl of apples.

At home, he hammered a nail into the wall, then carefully hung the painting of the woman with the apples above his bed, hooking the wooden frame onto the nail. He adjusted the painting until it was absolutely straight, then studied it for a long time.

Ramon took out his notebook and wrote:

Thurs., October 4.
The lady in Glasser's painting has a sad mouth because she got to live in my emty house with no lights. She's only made of paint so she's sad for always. If I tell a funny story, or tickle her face,

or sing, she can't smile. But if my mamá came home and sang, I bet the lady would smile like a miracle.

Ramon read over the words he'd written. Yeah, that's the truth, he thought. Like Glasser said, now I feel better. Even if what I wrote stinks, I still feel better.

10

The little goat bell tinkled as Ramon opened the door of the Colombian *bodega*, the grocery store around the corner from his apartment. At the sound of the bell, Mr. Herrera, the owner, appeared at the hanging drapes that closed off the back room. Ramon leaned the canvases against a large glass case holding milk, eggs, and beer. Above the case a sign read CERVEZA, beer.

"Qué pasa?" asked Mr. Herrera.

"Hey, Herrera!" called Ramon. "Look at these paintings. Ain't they great! You know what you need? You need a picture for your store, instead of that beer sign." Ramon tried to sound as confident as announcers he'd seen on TV commercials. "What do you think? *Muy bonitas,* hey? *Las mejores!*"

Mr. Herrera shrugged his shoulders. "That's not

pictures. That's junk. What is that, there? Is that a man? A tree? It's a lot of junk. . . . Did *you* paint that?"

"Naa. It's a friend of mine. He's a famous artist."

"*Sí, sí, sí!* Famous! Why does he need you to give away his paintings if he's such a famous artist, hey?"

"I ain't giving them away. I'm selling them. Fifty dollars each. But they're on sale for thirty dollars. They could become very valuable."

"Oh, *sí*. Then keep them yourself."

Ramon tried to remember a phrase he'd heard on the radio. "We need instant cash," he said. "So, you know, we're selling a few at a bargain sacrifice."

"Where did you steal them from, *chico*?"

"I didn't! This guy really gave me these to sell."

"I don't need pictures in a *bodega*."

"Hey, Herrera! My *mamá* bought plenty of stuff from you! We could have gone to the supermarket, but we came to *you*! I been here a million times. Now you oughta buy something from *us*!" Ramon's fists were clenched. All these years Mr. Herrera had always been friendly. But now! Now he's turning his back on me, he thought. Yeah, some friend. He'll take our money anytime.

"Hey look, *chico*. All you ever brought in here is food stamps—"

"It's the same as money!" shouted Ramon.

"Food stamps make more work for me! . . . Anyway, I don't need no painting—"

"You don't need *any* painting!"

"*Qué?*"

"What do you mean, *what?* I'll tell you *what!* If you don't want a painting, next time I'll go to Gomez's store. I don't need you!"

"Go! Go to Gomez! Go to hell! I don't want your food stamps. Tell your *mamá,* for me, that she's Puerto Rican so go to *una bodega puertorriqueña!*"

"This is the U.S.A., man! My *mamá* can go wherever she wants. She's *American,* man!"

"*Chico,* you can make believe with the paintings! But don't make believe with that! You think your *papá* is in jail for three years because he's an American? If he was an American, he'd be in jail for three months!"

"He hit a cop!"

"I *know* he hit a cop. . . . *Chico,* don't fight with me! I got enough problems! My wife's got the cancer, hey! What do I need a picture for! She's got the cancer, hey? *Hey?*"

"Cancer? . . . Oh . . . I didn't know that. . . . Uh . . . hey, Herrera, you know . . . you can have a painting for her for free—"

"I don't want a picture if you paid me to take it. Those pictures make me sick. *Enfermo!*"

"Yeah. OK. It's, like, you know, modern art. . . . Hey . . . I'll still buy stuff here, OK?"

"*Sí, sí, sí!* Good-bye!"

"*Sí. Hasta luego.*"

"Hasta luego? What happened to the *American?"*

"Hey, Herrera . . . I'm . . . you know . . . I'm sorry about your wife. You know?"

"Sure, sure, sure, I know. . . .

"Hasta luego, Señor Herrera . . . amigo."

"Amigo, eh? . . . *Adiós, Ramón Santiago . . . compadre!"*

Ramon gathered the paintings together. It felt good to hear his name pronounced the Spanish way again and to be called *compadre,* comrade. There were things that couldn't be said any other way but in Spanish. *Compadre* . . . Maybe Herrera meant that they were somehow close because they both had someone sick in the hospital. Could it mean that? Ramon wished he understood Spanish better, all the hidden things a word could mean. But even at home, he couldn't always understand what his mother or father was saying.

Ramon decided to try Mrs. Ryan's Pet Shop next. Mrs. Ryan had had her pet shop in the same broken-down store for over forty-five years. When Ramon was younger he would sometimes stand for an hour and watch the animals play and fight in the window. Some days Mrs. Ryan would put puppies in the window; other days, kittens or parrots or turtles. She had been doing it ever since Ramon could remember.

The door rattled on its ancient frame as Ramon walked in. There was a flurry in the cages along the walls, and instantly the shop was filled with birds calling and puppies yelping. Mrs. Ryan walked along the row of cages whispering *Hush . . . Hush . . . Hush* soothingly, while looking directly at Ramon.

"And what can I do for you, young man?" she asked. "Look at all them pictures you're carrying, now."

"Hey, Mrs. Ryan!" called Ramon. "You know what you need? A painting! Yeah. Look at these." He quickly leaned the paintings against a row of empty fish tanks. "A friend of mine, he painted these. Ain't they beautiful! They're for sale. Cheap!"

Mrs. Ryan squinted at the paintings amid a chorus of bird cries and yelping puppies. "There's nice colors to 'em," she said. "But I don't like 'em, not a bit. Whoever painted 'em is touched in the head for sure. Look at that man. He's blue. A blue man! I don't like 'em a bit."

Ramon scratched his head. "Yeah . . . You know, they're, like, what they call modern art."

"I'm not modern," said Mrs. Ryan. "Try Herrera next door. He plays all that dance music all day. Right through the wall; it disturbs my parakeets. He's modern, not me."

"Yeah," said Ramon. "Well thanks."

Ramon went two stores down, to the Bargain Discount Center. Mrs. Diaz was busily sorting out packets of socks in deep bins at the front of the store. The Discount Center always had something new to look at: candles shaped like animals, leftover party favors, sunglasses, clocks, ball-point pens, used comic books, anything and everything. Ramon sometimes bought used comic books, read them, then sold them back to Mrs. Diaz for a few cents less than he'd paid.

"Hey, Mrs. Diaz," said Ramon. "I got some paintings from a real artist. You could sell them in your store and make a lot of money. Look at this stuff."

Mrs. Diaz didn't look up from the socks. "I don't sell paintings. I sell pictures."

"Yeah, but these are good." Ramon placed them on top of the bins.

Mrs. Diaz stared at the paintings, then she shook her head. "That's no good for me. No good. People don't want that. They want pictures. Nice pictures. They don't want that. That's for rich people on Fifth Avenue."

"Yeah?"

"*Sí.* Not for Ninth Avenue. On Ninth Avenue, it has to be a nice picture."

Yeah, thought Ramon. Maybe she's right. . . . OK. I'll hustle them over on Fifth Avenue. People got a lot of money there. But I better change into my good pants for Fifth Avenue. And my good shirt. On Fifth Avenue you gotta dress good to hustle.

11

Ramon tugged at his pants as he walked. "They don't fit anymore," he murmured to himself. "If I bend over, I'll split them right down the rear. Last year they fit good. . . . I guess I'm taller. I ain't fatter, so I guess I'm taller."

He shifted the paintings to his other arm as he walked toward Fifth Avenue. Ramon felt uneasy; Fifth Avenue was someone else's territory, not his. His own avenues, Tenth Avenue, Ninth, Eighth, were as familiar as his living room. The cracked sidewalks littered with torn newspapers, beer cans, paper bags, and broken glass seemed as friendly to him as pigeons or squirrels in the park. And the people were always there. Men and women sitting on front steps or leaning out of windows; always there. As he walked, Ramon looked up and waved to an old woman staring at the street below. The woman waved back, her hand fluttering like the torn curtains in her window.

It all changed at Broadway. Broadway was a river to be crossed, dividing his city and the other. Ramon plunged into the crowd, edging the paintings between people, dancing away from near collisions. He quickly scanned the familiar Broadway confusion of street vendors, movies, record shops, adult book stores, taco stands, police, beggars, tourists, and teenagers like himself. Instantly, as a pilot reads his instruments, Ramon "read" Broadway.

Yeah, thought Ramon. These paintings are too good for Broadway. It's gotta be Fifth Avenue. The best! Nothing but the—

Ramon didn't finish his thought. Was that Angel over there, near the man handing out leaflets? It looked like him.

Ramon walked toward him. It *was* Angel. What's he doing on Broadway, wondered Ramon. Probably trying to sneak into one of them X movies, or something. Angel the Rat Killer. Rats and dirty movies, that's Angel. Why's he staring at me? He's seen the paintings, that's what.

As Ramon walked toward him, Angel ducked into the crowd and disappeared. Hey, that's weird, thought Ramon. He's gone!

Ramon walked a block down Broadway, then suddenly turned back. There was Angel, again, slipping behind a parked truck on the corner of Forty-eighth Street.

Oh man! He's following me, thought Ramon. I bet he followed me all morning. Harpo must've told him to. I should've reported back to them yesterday, and showed them the paintings right away. Yeah, I should've. I bet Angel thinks I stole these paintings for myself. I don't care what any of them think! I'm gonna sell these! I am! . . . Maybe I oughta talk to Angel. I ain't gonna let him bug me.

Ramon walked deliberately toward Angel at the far end of the block. I'm coming after you, Angel, he thought. Rat Angel, you ain't gonna bug me, man.

But Angel darted in and out of the crowds, always keeping a block ahead of Ramon. At Fifty-third Street, Ramon gave up and turned east toward Fifth Avenue again.

That stupid mother! Why don't he let me explain? Them guys don't have to worry. When I sell the paintings, I'm gonna split my half with them.

As Ramon walked east from Broadway toward the Museum of Modern Art, the buildings became white stone and shining glass. Along the Avenue of the Americas, great new hotels rose above plazas with graceful fountains and modern sculpture. Ramon had walked through the lobby of one of those hotels, once. Among the thick carpets and hushed lounges, he had felt the people staring at him, and had suddenly been ashamed of his clothing, of his face, of his very bones. Ashamed to be Puerto Rican. As he walked, the memory still felt sharp as a thorn.

He had reached Fifth Avenue. The sunlight slanted between white buildings and there was a dazzle upon everything: the crowds shopping and strolling, the flags rippling in the breeze, buses, cars. The air was alive with light.

Ramon hesitated, stepping back into the side street. I can't hustle here, he thought. No way. No way. . . . What would I say? What would I do? . . . I dunno. I dunno. . . .

Do it anyway, man! Put on an act! All them other hustlers do it!

Ramon walked quickly to the granite wall of a church facing Fifth Avenue and set up the canvases, five in a row, against the wall. Then he cupped his hands to his mouth and called, "Hey! Here it is, everybody! First time on Fifth Avenue! Check it out! Original paintings! Real paintings, not junk! Five original paintings! When these five go, there ain't no more! Check 'em out!"

A few passersby glanced at the paintings, but no one stopped. Jive, thought Ramon. Give them jive.

"Help a painter through art school! Help a painter get inside them museums! The Museum of Art's right down the block. Modern Art! Outside today, inside tomorrow! Only thirty dollars a painting! Tomorrow these paintings could be worth a million! You can't lose! You can only win! Hey! Hey!"

Several people stopped to look, and a well-dressed man picked up a painting and studied it.

"Look them over! The paint is in layers! You can see right through! Layer after layer! That's real art! Check 'em out!"

The man picked up another painting and examined it. Then he turned to Ramon. "Did I hear you say you painted these?"

Give him hype, thought Ramon. He *wants* me to have painted it. Who cares who painted it? If it's good, it's good. "Yeah, I did it," he said. "You like them?"

"You painted these? I don't believe it! Where did you get these, anyway?"

"Naa. I really painted them."

"How old are you?"

"Me. Ahh . . . fifteen."

"Painting like this at fifteen! Unbelievable!"

"Yeah, that's what my teachers all say. Unbelievable. That's what they say. So I figure, I'll sell a few, that way I can buy paint 'n' stuff. . . . You want one? It's only thirty dollars."

A small crowd had gathered by now. The man glanced at the crowd, then turned back to Ramon. "Glasser? Are you Glasser?"

"Huh?" Ramon answered.

"A. Glasser. The signature there. What does the *A* stand for?"

"Oh . . . Angel. Angelo Glasser, but I call myself Angel."

"Angelo Glasser? That's a pretty unusual combination, wouldn't you say?"

"Yeah. Well, you know, my father's Jewish and my mother's Catholic. So that's where that comes from."

"And you really painted these?"

"Yeah, sure."

"Hmm . . . Well . . . I may be crazy, but I'll take one."

"You got it!" Oh mama, oh mama, thought Ramon. I sold one in five minutes! Thirty bucks! Fifth Avenue, you are sweet! You are sweet, *sweet*, SWEET!

The man selected a yellow-and-gold painting of leaves, the one Glasser had said was his own self, laughing. Ramon suddenly wished the man had picked a different one; he could have kept this one for his mother.

As the man gave him three ten-dollar bills from his thick wallet, Ramon handed him the painting. Look at that, he thought. Flip, flip, flip. Three tens, just like that. The same way I pull off chewing gum wrappers. That's money, man! Dopey Luis, you're working on the wrong side of Manhattan! Wait'll I tell the gang. This is where they oughta do their jobs.

"Hey, hey!" called Ramon to the crowd. "Check

'em out! Original paintings! Send an art student through school! Thirty dollars now, tomorrow a million. Look at the colors! Blue! Green! Hey, lady, wouldn't you like one of these on your wall! Thirty small, tiny dollars for one big, fat painting. Check 'em out!"

Ramon spotted Angel again, a block away, standing, watching. What's the matter with him? thought Ramon. He oughta help me sell these. What does he think I'm doing, putting on a free show!

Then, just as suddenly, Angel was gone again. Weird, thought Ramon. That guy's really *loco*.

"Hey, hey!" he called again to the crowd. "Original paintings! Painted by me, a twelve-year-old kid. My teachers say I'm it! I'm the next Picasso! I'm the next Pedro Picasso! Thirty little dollars and you can own a genius!"

People watched a few minutes, smiling, curious, then walked off to be replaced by others. But no one bought any more paintings. Maybe it was just luck, thought Ramon. I better change my jive. Yeah, I'll try something else. But I gotta lose this crowd first.

Ramon picked up the four remaining paintings, walked around the block, then set them up again. The people who had been watching were gone.

"Hey, hey! Ladies and gentlemen! I got some paintings here that came from a guy in Europe. These are Russian paintings stolen in the big World War!

Russian paintings by Arbotsky Glasser! Look at these! Valuable! Rare! Russian paintings by the famous Arbotsky Glasser who they put in jail!"

A woman examined the paintings, carefully, then whispered something to the man with her.

"Arbotsky Glasser?" the woman asked. "I never heard of him."

"I know. He's just getting discovered now. 'Cause all his stuff was, like, you know, hidden. They had to smuggle it out."

"How did you get these, anyway?" asked the man.

"I dunno. My *papá* got them a long time ago. But they're real! These paintings are real!"

"I can see that," said the woman. "The influence of late Malevich is unmistakable. I'd love to know how your father got these. But I guess I'd better not ask. . . . These are very fine paintings. Very fine."

Ramon wished Glasser could hear the compliment. But he'd tell him; he'd tell him. *Very fine.* . . . Ramon did a quick calculation. Hey, good, he thought. The price just went up to sixty dollars. That's what *very fine* costs.

"Yeah, you know," said Ramon. "The only reason my *papá*'s selling these is 'cause he's out of a job. It's been tough. So they only cost . . . uh . . . seventy dollars each."

"Seventy?" The couple looked at each other with suppressed smiles, as if they'd discovered diamonds being sold as glass.

82

"Yes, I'd like that one," said the woman.

"And we'll have this one, too," said the man. "Will you take a check?"

"Oh . . . uh . . ." Ramon hesitated. "I'm sorry, but my *papá*, he said cash only."

"Well . . . Ellen, do you have thirty?" asked the man. "I know I started out with a hundred and ten dollars today."

The woman checked her handbag and counted her money. "All I have is eight dollars and we'll need that for a cab. Young man, we have exactly one hundred and ten dollars. Are you willing to sell two paintings for fifty-five dollars each?"

Ramon forced a frown. "Uh . . . well . . . I guess I could. Yeah, I guess I could. . . . OK. Fifty-five each."

Oh man, he thought. The money is pouring in. He pushed the bills deep into his pocket, beneath his knife.

"Hey! Hey! Check 'em out! Only two left! Arbotsky Glasser! Arbotsky Glasser! Painted in Russia and smuggled out!"

Ramon stood and called for over an hour. People stopped, looked for a moment, shook their heads, then moved on. No one bought another painting. The crowds in the street were thinning out and it was growing dark.

"Hey, hey . . ." I can't shout no more, thought Ramon. I'm getting hoarse. I better try something else, 'cause I sure ain't gonna carry these back to

Ninth Avenue. If I buy this one of the trees for my *mamá*, all I gotta do is sell that red one, and I'm done.

"Ladies and gentlemen," he said to the dwindling group of onlookers. "It's getting late and I gotta go home. So I'm gonna sell that red-and-orange painting of them buildings for like the highest bid. Who'll bid, say, five dollars? Five dollars? That's just so I can go home. Some people paid fifty-five dollars for a painting before, and if you were watching you'd know. OK? Who says five to start?"

"*Cinco,*" called a voice from behind the others. It was Angel.

"Yeah, uh . . . OK. Five. I got five. Who'll say seven?"

"Seven," said a man holding a briefcase.

"*Diez,*" said Angel in a flat voice.

"Yeah, hey. That's . . . that's good. I got ten, now. Ten. Who'll say twelve?" called Ramon.

What's Angel doing, he wondered. He's helping me get the price up, but he sounds mean. He's been hanging around all this time!

"Twelve," called the man.

"*Quince!*" called Angel, loudly.

"Yeah. Hey, fifteen! I got fifteen! Who'll say twenty?"

"Twenty," called the man with the briefcase. "And that's my last offer. You tell your friend in the crowd here, if he bids again, he can keep it. It's worth twenty, but no more. Take it or leave it."

There was silence in the crowd. "Twenty, once!" called Ramon, trying to imitate an auctioneer he'd seen in a movie. "Twice! Three times, and it's sold to the gentleman with the briefcase and glasses for twenty dollars, cash."

The man counted out the money and held it up. "First you give me the painting. Then I give you the money. I know you guys."

"Yeah. Go ahead. Take it. It's yours."

As the painting and money were exchanged, and the crowd dispersed, Angel moved closer. "Hey Angel, what's going on!" called Ramon. "You been following me all day, man!"

"Give me the money," said Angel.

"Money?" asked Ramon, not sure whether Angel wanted it for himself or for the gang.

"You been pushing money in your pocket all afternoon, you freak!"

Ramon's hand went to the pocket with the knife. He really looks mean, he thought. I don't like how he looks.

Ramon tried to sound businesslike. "Hey Angel. This is the way it is. Glasser only got paintings, see. No money. But he got a lot of paintings. I'm selling them, see? And we got a deal. He gets half, and I get half. OK? But what I keep, Dopey Luis and the gang gets half and they can split that like they always do. Tell them, OK?"

"Yeah, sure, I'll tell them! You freaking liar! You're gonna split your take with that guy! You never stop lying, man!"

"I'm gonna split it with him, yeah! I'm not holding out on you!"

"You better give us our money, Santiago! That old guy can shove it! You keep on acting like you and him are *buenos amigos*, like you're on his side, and you're gonna get cut, man."

"I can do what I freaking want!"

Ramon backed away. Quickly he took the roll of bills and counted off forty dollars. He folded the forty dollars and tossed them at Angel, then plunged his hand back into his pocket, grasping the knife again.

"That's forty for the gang. Give it to them. I got a hundred and sixty all together and that's half my share. Tell them! I'm on their side! Tell them!"

"OK, I'll tell them, man," said Angel, picking up the money. "Hey Santiago. You know what I did yesterday?"

"No," said Ramon.

"I caught a rat. I caught a rat and cut its freaking head off. Just like that. . . ."

"Oh yeah?" said Ramon, trying to appear indifferent, though he felt sick.

"Yeah. And maybe you're *next*, man. . . . See you soon, Santiago."

Ramon knew Angel could never match him with

a knife, not one-on-one. Angel was full of it!

"Hey, Angel, you got a better chance with a rat," Ramon said. "Rats, they don't carry no blade on them."

Angel was already at the corner, but just before turning into the side street, he pulled an object from his jacket pocket and held it up for Ramon to see. It was the severed head of a rat.

"See you real soon, you freak," Angel called.

Oh man, thought Ramon, feeling sick again. That guy's crazy enough to do anything. Oh man, oh man.

12

His mother lay sleeping on her side. The lights in the room had been dimmed; the visiting hours were over. But no one had stopped Ramon as he carried the remaining painting through the hospital corridors.

The room had a smell. Ramon sniffed near his mother's bed; it wasn't coming from there. Then he glanced at the bed opposite and winced. A woman lay asleep with her head off the pillow; all over the side of her bed and on the floor was vomit.

Ramon shuddered. Don't they ever clean up? Don't they ever come around?

Quickly he placed the painting on the sill next to his mother's bed, where she would see it when she awoke. It was a painting of trees in a dozen shades of green, the lush trees of Puerto Rico she'd described to Ramon so often.

"There," murmured Ramon. "Now you can be in Cataño."

The smell in the room seemed to grow worse. Ramon adjusted the painting, then turned and fled.

He raced down the corridor to the nurses' desk. "Hey! Hey, nurse!" he called. "In Room 718! A lady's thrown up all over everything. It smells in there! It smells bad!"

"The orderly's only got two hands," said the nurse.

"You give me a bucket and mop, *I'll* clean that stuff up!"

"Who do you think you are! It's past visiting time! We'll get to that as soon as we can."

Suddenly Ramon changed from anger to pleading, hoping it might help. "Please? My *mamá*, she's in that room. Please?"

"Who is your mother?"

"Santiago. Mrs. Santiago."

"Yes. All right. We'll get to that room soon. That's the least of our problems, vomit."

"Yeah. Yeah. Thanks."

Ramon took the elevator down, trying to think. Maybe he could do something with the money. Maybe he could bribe some of the nurses to look after his mother better. But there were so many of them: nurses, orderlies, doctors. And he never seemed to see the same nurse twice. How could you bribe so many?

Out on the street, Ramon hesitated. He wanted

to run somewhere, anywhere, to get away from that smell, from that room, from Angel.

He thought of Glasser. He could visit Glasser. He could go up to Eighty-fourth Street and give Glasser his part of the money, and maybe stay awhile and talk some more about his paintings, about his laughing in some paintings and crying in others. That would be good. Because Glasser could see things inside you, just like his mother could before she got sick. That would really be good. Ramon started walking uptown.

He slowed his pace as he passed a run-down restaurant on Fifty-ninth Street. A man was grilling some thin steaks behind the wide plate-glass window. The smell of broiled steak made Ramon's stomach squeeze with hunger. He watched the man flip the steaks with a spatula, then toss sliced onions onto the grill.

That's what I want, he thought. Steak and onions. I can eat steak now 'cause I'm rich. Hey, *muy bien!* I'm gonna celebrate selling the paintings and go up to Glasser later. . . . Or wait . . . hey, wait . . . I could buy some steaks and junk in the supermarket and bring it all up there. We could both celebrate. He said I ain't never coming back. I'll show him! I'm gonna get the two biggest steaks I can find!

Yeah, but what if Angel sees me. Or Harpo. . . . Shit, I can do what I feel like! I'm giving them half my money! I can eat steak with anybody I want!

Them freaks! . . . Still, I better not let them see me go up there. . . .

Near Seventy-second Street, Ramon found a food market that was still open. In a whirl through the store, he filled a shopping cart with steaks, frozen French fried potatoes, a bottle of ketchup, onions, a gallon container of milk, three boxes of chocolate cookies, a loaf of bread, a pound of butter, and a dozen eggs. Now he can have eggs for breakfast, thought Ramon.

With a bag in each arm, Ramon walked up Amsterdam Avenue to Eighty-fourth Street as fast as he could, looking behind every so often to make sure no one was following him. Mama, I'm hungry, he thought. Steak and onions! I'm gonna fall dead from hunger before I get there.

At the apartment building, Ramon took one last look up and down the block. No one. He pressed Glasser's button with his elbow, still hugging both bags of food. The buzzer sounded and Ramon pushed his way into the lobby. I'm beginning to feel like I live here, he thought. Yeah, it'd be nice to live here. A carpet in the lobby whenever I went home. That carpet smells good.

In front of Glasser's apartment door, Ramon had a sudden idea. He'd pretend he was delivering groceries. He tapped on the door with his foot, the bags still in his arms.

"Who?" asked Glasser from behind the door.

"Delivery! Hansen's Market!" said Ramon.

"What? I didn't order anything," Glasser called. "Try Costanza, next door."

Suddenly Ramon flushed. I did it, he thought. I did it! I just gave the whole thing away. Glasser can figure out that Dopey Luis was in on the robbery. I screwed it all up! . . . Act like it was nothing. . . .

"Hey Glasser, I'm just kidding. It's me, remember? Ramon. Your painting salesman. I sold 'em. I got money and I got steaks. Lemme in; I'm starving!"

With a rattling of chains and locks, Glasser opened the door.

"So you're back! . . . Hey, why all those groceries?"

"I got steaks! All kinds of stuff! I'm gonna make us dinner. We're gonna celebrate! Come on, man, lemme in!"

"So come in. Nobody's stopping you. . . . Did you really sell the paintings?"

"Sure! You gotta have faith, man!" Ramon dropped the bags of food on the kitchen table, then took out his roll of bills. "I owe you eighty—and say, twenty for the painting for my *mamá*—you get a hundred dollars. How's that!"

"Put it on the table," said Glasser, waving his hand at the money. "And take all these groceries out of it."

"Naa. You can pay for the next one."

"You really sold them, eh? You didn't get this money . . . somewhere else?"

92

"No! I sold them! I didn't rob nobody!"

Glasser nodded several times, deep in thought. "So you've really come back. Well, well, well, well, well . . . Maybe I've won my own bet. . . ."

"Hey Glasser, I'm hungry. How about like you go inside and paint or something. I'm gonna make us steak and onions and everything. OK?"

"Are you sure you know how to cook a steak?"

"Yeah. What d'ya think I am, dumb?" Ramon wondered if he really could. He tried to recall how the man in the restaurant window had flipped the steaks.

"It would be criminal to ruin a good steak," said Glasser, pointing toward the bags on the table.

"Hey, maybe I don't know what's in all them books, OK? But I know what I know, and I know how to make a freaking steak!"

"OK, wise guy. Call me when dinner is served. . . ." Glasser remained at the kitchen door, shaking his head in disbelief. "I don't know. I don't know. . . . Why do I feel this is all another trick? I still believe you're going to take that knife out yet. I believe it."

"Yeah. You're right!" In a great sweep, Ramon took the knife from his pocket and held it upright, blade in the air. "Only thing is, I'm gonna use it to cut the steaks up. So get into the freaking living room and lemme cook . . . wise guy!"

13

While Ramon sat at the kitchen table finishing the last of his steak, Glasser ran hot water into the frying pan at the sink, then wheeled back to the table. Holding his steak bone like a giant sparerib, Ramon gnawed at every crevice, hunting for bits of meat. Glasser held up a French fried potato.

"You know something. You're just about the hungriest fifteen-year-old—"

"Fourteen," said Ramon.

"Fourteen-year-old I've ever seen, including myself," said Glasser, "and I was pretty hungry sometimes. But I'm luckier than you, because I'm old and hungry, and I'll be finished with this whole stinking world soon. But you! You're *young* and hungry. I don't envy you. You have a lifetime of hunger ahead. All kinds of hunger. The older you get the better off you are. That much less hungriness ahead.

Yes, I'm old enough to feel sorry for you because you're young. What do you think of that?"

"Hey, you're old all right," said Ramon, still holding his steak bone. "You really are. Maybe you oughta drink some milk. It's good for you."

Glasser slammed the table angrily. "Listen, I don't need you telling me to drink milk! You think I'm old? Take my hand! Here, hold it!" Glasser held his right hand out.

Ramon hesitated, then held Glasser's hand. Slowly, firmly, Glasser began to squeeze.

"OK, try to get out of it," said Glasser, pressing harder. "See what you can do."

Ramon tried to squeeze back, but Glasser's hand was like an iron clamp. Ramon's hand burned, then felt numb.

"Hey, OK," said Ramon. "OK, man, OK! Let go!"

Glasser released his grip. "How's that! That will teach you to tell me about drinking milk as if I'm some kind of creaky antique."

"Yeah, hey, you're strong!"

"You think just because a man has arthritis in the legs, he's finished? Well I'm not finished! Arnold Glasser is never finished!"

"Hey Arnold Glasser, I got news for you. Ramon Santiago is never finished either!" said Ramon. "I bounce back! Shake!" Ramon held his hand out toward Glasser.

Glasser pushed his empty plate into Ramon's outstretched hand. "That's the spirit. Here. You can put this in the sink for me if you want to bounce back, Mr. Ramon Santiago. . . . So that's your last name. Santiago, hey? Ramon Santiago. A good name. I like it."

"Well I hate to tell you," said Ramon as he collected the other dishes, "but Arnold Glasser *ain't* good. It don't sell no paintings. On Fifth Avenue your name's Arbotsky. Arbotsky Glasser. That's jive, man. That's what people want: jive."

"I'm sure it is," said Glasser bitterly. "It's taken me a lifetime to see what you see at fourteen. How sad for me. Or maybe for you. I'm not sure."

"Me neither. . . . Hey Glasser. Who's this guy, Marvel-vich?"

"What?"

"Some Russian painter. Marvel-vich."

"Malevich! How could you have heard of Malevich?"

"Some people that bought your paintings said your stuff reminds them of—Malay-vich?"

Glasser looked thoughtful. "My paintings have absolutely nothing to do with Malevich. We're complete opposites. Still, those people at least heard of him. That's something. . . ."

"Yeah. They think your stuff is great! They acted like I was dumb selling it. Like it was really valuable. Like it was by Pedro Picasso or somebody."

"Picasso's work sells for up to a million dollars,

wise guy! But . . . I must admit, I did think my work had some value once. Once . . . a long time ago . . . Maybe I'll show you something. Why not? Come on, Mr. Ramon Santiago. It's in the living room."

Glasser wheeled into the living room and started searching among his bookshelves. "Where did it go? . . . Where? . . . Wait, here it is."

He took out a large book with a title in black: *Despair and Hope: The Painters of the 1930's*. "This is what I used to be, before I became nothing," he said as he opened the book. "I haven't shown this to anybody for years. . . . I shouldn't even show it to you. . . . But since you're my official art salesman— Anyway, let's see what you think."

Ramon studied a color photograph of a huge mural painted on the wall of an auditorium. In the mural, dozens of eager men, women, and children poured in a great throng from a subway station to the street, their eyes fixed on something beyond them. In small print below the photograph was the title *Tomorrow*, and the words: *Arnold Glasser, Auditorium, New York Institute of the Social Sciences, 1936*. Even in the photograph, Ramon could detect the layers of color that appeared in all of Glasser's paintings.

"That's great!" said Ramon.

"Turn the page," said Glasser.

Ramon saw a mural of farmers, men and women, binding sheaves in a field of dazzling yellow wheat.

97

Below, the printing read: *Iowa Gold Rush, Arnold Glasser, Great Hall, Iowa State College, 1938.*

"Turn!"

In the next mural, dozens of children of every race and nationality, in their native costumes, were stretching, hanging, sitting on the climbing bars in a playground. Below were the words: *Peace Plan, Arnold Glasser, The Children's Clinic, Baltimore, Maryland, 1940.*

Oh mama, thought Ramon. He was a famous painter.

"What do you think?" asked Glasser.

"It's—it's *magnífico!*"

"*Magnífico*, eh? I wish you'd been one of the art critics back then. Maybe I wouldn't be a nobody today. Well . . . that's who I once was. . . ."

"You still are!"

Glasser gave a bitter laugh. "Not anymore. No one knows my paintings even exist anymore."

"What d'ya mean! *I* do!"

"Oh, of course. For selling in the streets to make a few dollars, right?"

"Hey, come on, Glasser! I hung your painting of the blue lady up over my bed. . . . OK! Wait! I got something for you." Ramon took out his notebook, flipped through the pages, and tore one out. He dropped the sheet in Glasser's lap. "See. This proves I know your paintings exist!"

Glasser read the sheet slowly, then murmured,

" 'But if my *mamá* came home and sang, I bet the lady would smile like a miracle.' . . ." Glasser studied the page again, then nodded his head. "Let me tell you, this is *magnífico*, too . . . *muy magnífico*, do I say that right? . . . I put myself into that painting. And you've put yourself into this. I can feel it." Glasser held out the sheet to Ramon. "Thank you for letting me read it. . . ."

"Hey, you can keep it. It's yours. Your painting made me write it, you know?"

"Thank you. Thank you for this gift." Glasser carefully folded the paper and slipped it into his wallet. "Punk kid! You really make me feel like Picasso, instead of a flop."

"You ain't no flop," said Ramon. "You just should've called yourself Arbotsky back then, that's all. Then you would've been as big as Pedro Picasso. Bigger!"

Glasser sniffed out a bitter laugh. "You're probably right. Where were you when I needed you, wise guy?"

"I'm here. You need me now."

"Don't be so sure!" said Glasser, sitting straight up, defiantly. "You need me more than I need you! *Pedro* Picasso? It's *Pablo* Picasso, friend!"

"Hey, that's right."

"Have you ever seen a painting by Picasso?"

"I dunno. Yeah! I seen some in a bookstore the other day."

"How about Matisse? Or Cézanne? Or Rembrandt?"

"I heard of Rembrandt. . . . Yeah, I heard of him."

Glasser grasped the sides of his wheelchair. "Heard of! You heard of Rembrandt! You can *see* twenty Rembrandt paintings in the Metropolitan Museum of Art, right here in New York. Right across the park! Why hear of? See! Go! Look! Taste!"

"Naa. That's like school."

"Punk! Punk! Have you ever been inside the Metropolitan?"

"Naa . . . I never went."

"OK! Tomorrow is Saturday! The Metropolitan Museum of Art opens at 10 A.M. You get here at nine! We're going to the Met! I haven't been there for a long time. And now I have a wheelchair pusher. You! And you have a guide to Western Civilization. Me! A deal?"

"Yeah, but I wanna sell some more of your stuff tomorrow—"

"Who needs it! We have enough money for now. We've fed the stomach. Now let's feed the soul! Yes?"

"Yeah . . . but the stomach's gonna get hungry again tomorrow."

"So is the soul. If I have to choose, let the stomach go to hell. I've stood and cried, yes cried, in front of a painting by El Greco in my time, but I've never cried in front of a steak. You have to make choices.

Which do you want to feed? The stomach or the spirit? Which?"

Ramon thought a moment, then said firmly, "I wanna feed both. Yeah, that's it. Both."

"Not a bad answer," said Glasser. "Sane and balanced. Unlike me. OK, wise guy, tomorrow you're going to meet Mr. Rembrandt. Get here by nine A.M."

"Naa."

"What do you mean: *Naa*?"

"I ain't gonna get here by nine 'cause I'm gonna sleep over here tonight. OK?"

"Sleep over here? . . ."

"Don't worry! I ain't gonna knife you in the middle of the night. It's just . . . I dunno. I don't feel like going home. There's nobody around. You know?"

"What about your father? Doesn't he care where you are?"

"He's . . . he's away."

"What? Isn't he there when your mother is sick? What kind of a man is he?"

"Well . . . he's in Attica. You know, upstate? The prison? He hit a cop during a rally for Puerto Rico. He's been gone almost a year."

"I see . . . I see. . . . They say Attica's pretty tough."

"Yeah. They sent him to the worst place, 'cause it was a cop he hit. But the cop started it!"

"I see. . . . Your father sounds like he believes

in something. I've been in a few rough-and-tumble rallies in my time, too. . . . Anyway, you can sleep here anytime you want. Anytime."

"Naa, it's just tonight. Like, there's some guys I don't wanna meet tonight, and it's late, and I'm tired and—"

"Enough! You don't need reasons. Sleep over here whenever you like."

"Thanks. Thanks a lot. . . . Can I use that couch there?"

"The couch is yours. Go! Sleep your head off!"

"Hey, OK!" said Ramon, "Go! The bedroom is yours! Sleep your head off, too."

"Wise guy."

"Yeah, that's me."

14

Morning light moved across Ramon's face as he opened his eyes and stretched. He was in a strange room. Where? Instantly, he felt for his knife.

There was a smell of hot fat from the kitchen and a spattering sound. He remembered. Glasser sure gets up early, he thought as he sank back onto the couch.

At the half-open window, a breeze lifted the lace curtains. The shadow of the curtains moved on the nearby wall. The filigreed shadow rose and settled and rose again, dark flecks on a sea of heaving light. Ramon watched the pattern of shadows rise and stretch and fall, again and again. Hey, that's good, he thought. I never saw that before. . . . It makes it look like the wall is moving.

Ramon pulled out the book and stubby pencil from his pocket, found a clean page, and wrote:

Saturday, October 6.
Glasser got these curtins. They make a shadow like
a lepard walking smooth. There it goes again.

As Glasser appeared in the hallway, Ramon
pushed the book into his pocket.

"So you're finally awake! Good morning!" Glasser
said in a booming voice.

"Yeah, good morning."

"It's almost afternoon! Ten-thirty-five. How can
anybody sleep until ten-thirty-five?"

"I dunno. Hey, what're you cooking?" asked Ramon, as he felt a sudden pang of hunger.

"See! Hungry again! It never ends! . . . I'm making eggs. Sunny-side up. How many for you, one
or two?"

"Uhh . . . three," said Ramon.

"Three?"

"Yeah . . . or make it four, OK? I dunno, I had
all that steak last night, but I'm still starving."

"Four eggs and leftover French fried potatoes.
How's that?"

"Yeah!"

"OK, wise guy. Fill up now, because you're going
to walk your head off, pushing me around town.
You'll need four eggs, believe me."

Glasser returned to the kitchen and Ramon heard
the crack of eggs against the edge of the frying pan.
The sound made him hungrier. A quick, nervous

breeze from the window bellied out the curtains into a pair of sails. Hey, those curtains are good stuff, he thought.

He went to the window and shook the curtains, then bunched them to see what kind of shadow they would throw on the wall. Then he glanced out the window; it was much higher than his own apartment. Seven stories below, the Saturday traffic of Eighty-fourth Street moved slowly by. Ramon watched two girls tossing a Frisbee back and forth; it looked like a small orange dot floating between them above the sidewalk. A delivery boy on a three-wheeled bicycle watched the girls from the far corner. Every so often he looked up toward Glasser's apartment. Ramon wondered if it could be Dopey Luis; the food store he worked for, Hansen's Market, was only a few blocks away.

He suddenly tensed, touching his knife by reflex. If that *was* Dopey Luis, then they were still following him. They knew he was in Glasser's apartment! Ramon bunched the curtain again and moved it in front of his face.

"Breakfast!" Glasser called from the hallway. "Hey, watch those curtains! Very delicate stuff. My wife made those. . . . It was the year she died."

"Jeez, I'm sorry," Ramon said, moving away from the window.

"You don't have to be sorry," said Glasser quietly. "It was twenty years ago. Twenty years, and I'm still painting her. . . . The painting you have, the blue lady, that's her, too. . . . Twenty years . . ." Glasser seemed lost in his thoughts. Then he suddenly slapped his hands together and called with a forced cheerfulness, "Come on! Come on! Get your eggs before I eat them all myself! Let's go!"

"OK, I'm coming!" Ramon called back. He took one last look at the delivery boy, then went to the kitchen.

During breakfast, Ramon poured glass after glass of milk for himself, while Glasser sipped a huge mug of coffee.

"Drink your milk, little boy," said Glasser, teasingly. "It's good for you, sonny. It'll make you big and strong like me, sonny."

"*Sí, sí, Señor Loco,*" Ramon answered. "*Señor Loco Viejo.*"

"That sounds like *old lunatic* to me," said Glasser.

"Yeah, sounds like it to me, too," said Ramon.

"That's all I needed. A wise guy in my kitchen."

After breakfast, Glasser shaved and put on a clean shirt. Then he pushed clothing around in his bureau till he found a brown sweater.

"There," he said, as he checked himself in a mirror on the bedroom wall. "Nothing but the best for the Metropolitan Museum of Art. Maybe I should wear my old silk scarf. . . . No. Too much! . . . All right, I'm ready. Let's go! Let's go!"

Glasser wheeled himself out to the elevator, but

in the lobby Ramon had to help him work the wheelchair out the door, down a step, and into the street. Ramon kept back behind the wheelchair and looked up and down the block, searching for the delivery boy. The girls were still tossing the Frisbee, but the delivery boy was gone.

"Let's get going, Mister Steak and Eggs," said Glasser. "Not so slow. We want to head south, then through Central Park. The scenic route by the lake. Mush! Mush!"

"What's mush?" asked Ramon.

"That's what they say to the huskies, the sled dogs, when they want them to pull the sleds. Right?"

"Oh yeah."

"So mush, wise guy. Mush!"

Ramon pushed the wheelchair along Central Park West, then started across the park, along one of the winding footpaths. They reached the first uphill section.

"Hey Glasser, this is tough work," said Ramon. "What you need is an engine on this thing."

"I *have* an engine on this thing. A new invention. It's called the Santiago engine. Very efficient. It runs on French fried potatoes. The only trouble is, it talks back."

"That's good. Hey Glasser, you're funny," said Ramon as he pushed the wheelchair to the top of the rise.

"Of course! Why shouldn't I be? If you don't

laugh, you cry. And then you're finished. You can cry forever, the way the world is."

"Yeah, that's what happened to this friend of mine. He cried himself to death."

"He what?" asked Glasser.

"He cried and cried, and all these tears came out, and he got drier and drier, and finally what happened is, he turned completely into dust, he was so dry. Like powdered milk. Yeah. From nothing but crying. We keep him in a flour box now and my *mamá*, before she went into that hospital, she made a lot of lemon cookies outa him. You know, 'cause the tears left the dust tasting like bitter lemon. See?"

"What an imagination!" said Glasser. "That sky full of surprises didn't come from nowhere, hey? . . . Why are we going so slowly?"

"Another hill."

"What hill? Mush, punk!"

"OK, OK! . . . *Señor Viejo*."

As they moved across the park, Glasser looked at everything eagerly. He pointed to some trees turning orange-red and called out, "Stop here a minute. Look! Look at those trees! I've seen this sight a million autumns, but I still want more. See what I mean about hunger? It never ends."

Ramon remembered how his mother loved to see the trees in autumn. But men, men never talked this way. His father never did. If you were macho, you could notice the animals in the zoo, but not trees turning color. Were artists different? Ramon knew *he* was different. Well maybe he really was an artist, just like Glasser. Maybe . . . But could you be an artist and be macho, too?

"It's almost a crime to go indoors to a museum on a day like this," said Glasser. "The real stuff is here. But we can do both. On to Rembrandt and company! Forward march . . . or I should say, forward mush!"

Ramon started pushing the wheelchair again. It was turning out to be a great Saturday, like the Saturdays he used to spend with his father, before he had become so angry all the time.

Then Ramon saw Dopey Luis. Dopey Luis on his three-wheeled delivery bike.

Dopey Luis nodded his head up and down, again and again, as if to say: *I see you*, or *I know what you're doing*. Then he dipped his hand into his pocket and raised his knife straight up in the air. With the knife held high, Dopey Luis threw Ramon a kiss in slow motion with his other hand. The kiss was an invisible arrow aimed at Ramon.

Another second, and Dopey Luis turned and pedaled away. They're out to get me, thought Ramon. They're out to get me! I didn't do nothing! I gave them money! And I'm gonna give them more. But I can do what I want. If I wanna push an old guy's wheelchair, I'm gonna! They ain't gonna scare me! They think they can follow me around and scare me, but they ain't gonna!

Oh mama, oh mama, they ain't gonna.

15

They had to enter the museum through a side entrance because of the wheelchair.

"Next time," said Glasser, "when you come by yourself, go in the main entrance up all the steps. Then you'll get the full works! Then you'll see what a fantastic building this is! Fantastic!"

They went up an elevator. In a moment, they were in an enormous hallway with statues and green plants everywhere. Light from the panels above seemed to be coming from the sky itself.

"Cyprus," said Glasser. "Ancient Cyprus. These statues are over two thousand years old. And they all resemble my Uncle Max, may he rest in peace."

"Hey, their hats all look like acorns," said Ramon.

"So they do! Maybe they *are* acorns. Who can tell? That's the spirit! Don't start worshiping art!

Make it a living thing! That's good."

They went up another elevator and came out among Chinese vases in delicate shades of blue, green, and red-brown. They reminded Ramon of his mother's old dishes that had faded with endless washing to a warm glow of hazy flowers.

"Now," said Glasser, "what do you think of this?" They stood before a huge statue of a man with a great sword in one hand and a severed head, held by its hair, in the other. *Perseus Holding the Head of Medusa* was printed beneath. Ramon thought of Angel holding up the rat's head. Then, with a shudder, he imagined his own severed head in Angel's hand.

"How do you like it?" Glasser asked.

"That guy's holding that chopped-off head like it's a bowling ball. I'll bet all the little kids really like that. Yeah. Terrific for nightmares."

"It's from a famous myth! A Greek myth. It isn't meant to frighten you. It's meant to make you feel the power of the moment in the story. As a catharsis. A purging."

"I don't know what all that is. And I'll bet the little kids don't either. But I'll bet they get good nightmares anyway."

Glasser slammed the sides of his wheelchair. "What should be done! Should they hide a great work of art in the basement because some children will get nightmares?"

"Yeah, they should. They got enough other stuff to show."

"Hmmph!" Glasser sank back in his wheelchair, totally exasperated.

"You want my opinion, right? You got it!"

"Some opinion."

"Yeah, 'cause you only want *your* opinion. Long as I say what you want, then it's OK!"

"Hmm . . ." Glasser thought a moment, then nodded. "Good. Very good. You *should* stand up for your opinion. I respect you for it. Don't let me buffalo you. . . . Still . . . do museums really have to worry about little kids? I never thought."

In the next room Ramon wheeled Glasser over to a painting of Columbus. "Hey, I know that! Yeah! That was in our history book in junior high. Hey, that's famous."

"I'll tell you something," said Glasser. "Years ago, when I first saw that painting, I thought the same thing, exactly. It was in my history book, too."

Ramon rubbed his finger on the varnished surface of the painting.

"Don't!" Glasser called out.

"Hey, it feels smooth. Your paintings feel rough."

"You're not supposed to touch anything here! They'll throw us out!"

Ramon rubbed the painting again. "It feels just like hard glue," he said.

"Listen, Ramon Santiago! If you touch one more

painting, our trip is over! I mean it! Maybe you're right about chopped-off heads, but *I'm* right about touching paintings!"

"OK."

"Good!"

"You get pissed easy, don't you," said Ramon.

"I don't like that expression!"

"There you go again!"

"Enough! Mush on!"

"Mush on, yourself, man! I ain't no Eskimo dog!"

"Are you going to have a fight with me, right here in the middle of the Metropolitan Museum of Art?"

"Yeah, if you keep saying mush."

"I said it all morning, and you seemed to like it. It's a little joke! That's all!"

"Not when you're pi— angry, it ain't!"

"I'm not angry!"

"The hell you ain't!"

"Look, why don't you go around the museum by yourself. I can wheel myself around. You think I'm turning you into an Eskimo dog, go!"

"OK, Glasser! I can read what's under the pictures just as good as you!"

"Fine!" Glasser spun around in the wheelchair and sped off to another room. Man, he's weird, thought Ramon. One minute, he's happy, the next minute he's sore. What'd I do! I touched a painting, that's all. I touch his paintings all the time. Besides,

I said I won't do it no more. Well, I can see this stuff without him. I don't need him.

Ramon stared at the Columbus portrait again, then walked to the next room. On one wall was an enormous painting of horses, horses being led in a great circle, with a crowd watching. The horses were so real, Ramon felt he could almost smell them and hear their whinnying. He read the title: *The Horse Fair* by Rosa Bonheur. Hey, thought Ramon. I never knew a lady could paint like that! I don't need no Glasser to explain this to me!

Ramon wandered from room to room. There were paintings of children by Hoppner and Raeburn and Reynolds. All the children looked rich, and all had pink cheeks and light-brown hair. I'll bet *they* never had roaches, thought Ramon.

As he continued, the paintings grew darker. Vermeer. Van Dyck. Ruisdael. And then, Rembrandt.

There were Rembrandt paintings everywhere. Men and women looking stiff and formal in their fluted white collars, like thick white platters enclosing their necks. And a man in a high turban, old and jovial. Glasser in a good mood, thought Ramon. Next, a young man, Rembrandt's son Titus. And then a self-portrait of Rembrandt himself, old and tired and sad. Glasser. Glasser at his worst. Glasser saying kill me, end it already.

Ramon studied the portrait and tried to see how Rembrandt had painted it. The brushstrokes swirled together, light, dark, brown, yellow, swirled as if they had been put on the canvas without thought, without effort. The way rain fell. The way Glasser's curtains rose in the breeze. I wish I could write stuff down the way Rembrandt paints, thought Ramon.

"That, in my opinion, is the greatest work of art in this museum. One of the greatest in the world." It was Glasser. He had wheeled silently next to Ramon.

"Mmm," murmured Ramon, sullenly. Glasser was trying to make peace. OK, he'd make peace, too. Maybe! Tomorrow or the next day. Maybe.

"That's what art's all about. Look how Rembrandt's eyes seem at the edge of tears. His first wife dead! His second wife dead! His son Titus dead! Everyone he loved dead! Yet here I am, his painting says. I'm finished. There's nothing left. But I stand firm. This is me! Take it or leave it! . . . What do you think? Can you see that in his eyes?"

Ramon wondered if he should give in and talk to Glasser. He stared at the painting without looking toward the wheelchair. The sad, lonely face in the painting was so alive. Yes, this one face was better than all those horses in that huge painting. So clear and quiet and sad. He looked at Glasser; Glasser was equally sad.

"So," said Glasser. "No answer. No answer is an answer, too."

Ramon remembered how his father wouldn't talk

to him after they'd had a fight. Sometimes for hours, or even days. But Glasser had come over and was talking right now. In a sudden burst, Ramon decided to end the silence.

"Hey, you know," he said. "I wish this guy Rembrandt could've known he'd be so famous. Maybe it would've made him happy. You think he knew, like, that this was such a great painting?"

"I don't think so. When an ugly caterpillar becomes a beautiful butterfly, does it know? It just becomes. That's what this is. The same."

"Yeah . . . Hey, Glasser. You're not so dumb, you know?"

"Coming from a fourteen-year-old to a seventy-six-year-old, I take that as a high compliment. Shake, kid."

Glasser seemed happy again, with the eager look he'd had in the park. He held out his hand toward Ramon, and Ramon took it. Then Glasser squeezed harder and harder as he'd done at dinner. Ramon winced.

"OK! OK, man!"

Glasser released his grip. "That's to remind you that seventy-six today is younger than fifty-six in Rembrandt's time. That's because we eat more spinach. All right, I want you to see one more Rembrandt over there. It's called *Aristotle Contemplating a Bust of Homer.*"

Ramon studied the painting of a richly dressed

man with one hand resting on the statue of a blind poet. The man wore a heavy gold chain that glowed in a flood of yellow light.

"Hey, that's good stuff. That looks like real gold. But who's this Aristotle and Homer?"

"Homer was the greatest poet of ancient Greece. The *Iliad* and *Odyssey*. Didn't they teach you about Homer in school?"

"I don't go there much," said Ramon. "School stinks. All it's good for is for hanging out so you can meet your friends. Stuff like that."

"Then how will you ever learn about that or that or *that*?" said Glasser angrily as he gestured from painting to painting. "From hanging out?"

"Well I ain't gonna learn it in school. You can't even hear the teacher half the time—"

"Then hear him the other half! . . . Look, I don't care what you do! I'm not your truant officer! You want to be a punk? Be a punk! But I'm not giving you any more paintings to sell!"

"Hey come on, Glasser . . ."

"Our deal is off."

"Come on . . ."

"I'm blackmailing you, plain and simple."

"OK! OK! I'll go! . . . OK?"

"Very good. And you get five more paintings to sell as your reward. Let's shake on it." Glasser extended his hand toward Ramon.

"Not me!" Ramon pulled his hand back.

117

"Too bad. OK, wise guy, I think we've had enough art for one day. And enough fighting. Push me home, but let's take the scenic route again. And maybe we'll stop for hot dogs and soda in the park. . . . Mush, wise guy, mush!"

"Hot dogs! Hey, yeah!"

"Always hungry. It never ends. Never."

16

Ramon sat glumly, staring at the blackboard. The math teacher, Mr. Corsio, thumped his desk with the palm of his hand, but the chatter of students continued.

"Hey gang! Stifle!" called Mr. Corsio. "Now do you all understand angle, side, angle? I challenge anybody to come up to the board and draw a triangle different from this one, with the same angle, side, angle. Anybody!"

"Hey, Mr. Corsio!" a boy in the back of the room called. "How much you gonna pay me if I do?"

"All right! I'll give anyone a dollar who can come up and draw a triangle noncongruent to this one with the same angle, side, angle."

"Hey, you're cheap, man," the boy called. "You can't hardly even buy a joint for a buck no more."

"One dollar," said Mr. Corsio. "Take it or leave it."

The boy walked up to the board, took the chalk, and started to sketch a handgun. There was laughter throughout the classroom. Man, I can't learn anything, thought Ramon. It's boring anyhow, all this stuff about stupid triangles. I know all this junk. I know it in two seconds and he keeps saying the same thing again and again.

"What has that gun got to do with geometry?" Mr. Corsio asked the boy at the board.

"That's the gun I'm gonna point at you, if you don't gimme the dollar," said the boy.

"Is that a threat?" Mr. Corsio asked, his voice rising. "Do you want me to call the police officer outside? Do you want me to give him your name, Johnson?"

"That ain't my name, man!" The class roared with laughter.

Corsio's crazy, thought Ramon. He don't know how to do anything. He's letting them kick him around! I'm getting out of here. This is gonna be my last class today. The hell with Glasser. I'm gonna sell more paintings. Maybe up in Central Park. I like that park. Hey, yeah! All the rich ladies go in the park, right near the zoo.

Ramon slid out of his seat and, with his books under his arms, walked toward the door.

"Where do you think you're going?" asked Mr. Corsio.

"I gotta go to the bathroom, bad," said Ramon, apologetically.

"He needs another popper," someone called out.

"Why are you taking all your books?" Corsio asked.

"He needs them for toilet paper," called a boy. " 'Cause there ain't none in the booths."

Ramon walked rapidly down the corridor to the building exit. In front of the school and across the street, he saw groups of teenagers bantering with one another, staging mock fights, dancing to music from portable radios. Their books lay on the sidewalk in random piles. Some were smoking cigarettes and a few were smoking joints.

Ramon searched among the crowd to see if anyone in Harpo's gang was there. Not gonna let them sneak up behind *me*, he thought. . . . Naa, they ain't here. They never come around the school. Safest place in the world, around the school.

Then Ramon spotted Felipe standing by himself, with a bundle of books under his arm. He was squinting in the sun, watching the dancers at a distance. Book-Eyes, thought Ramon. Always all alone. Yeah. Just like me. Ramon felt a sudden closeness to Felipe.

"Hey, Felipe!" he called. "Hey! How come you're cutting? You ain't supposed to be out here. Not you."

"Hey, Ramon!" Felipe called back. "You got books! You're carrying books! I don't believe it!"

Ramon moved his books up and down. "Yeah,

I'm trying to develop my arms. You gotta carry weights all day, like this. . . . What are you doing out here with the good guys, man?"

"It's gym. I hate gym. Hey, how come you ran outa that bookstore the other day? What happened?"

"Oh that. . . . There's this guy I had to meet, you know? And I saw the clock in the bookstore and I was late. Did you get your book?"

"Yeah. . . . Hey, I got another one. My father got it in a used-book store. It's real good. It shows all kinds of operations. Wanna see it after school?"

"Naa."

"It's got these pictures in it. Heart, lungs, everything, the way it looks while they're operating. In color."

Now it's hearts and lungs, thought Ramon. No wonder the guys think he's weird. They don't see he's smart. All they see, he's weird. He don't even need a knife, he's so weird. He's out of it.

"Hey Felipe," said Ramon, "how about cutting the rest of the day and help me sell some paintings in the park?"

"Paintings? You been painting?" asked Felipe.

"Naa, I didn't paint 'em. Some old guy I know, he's a good painter and I'm selling them for him. Come on, let's go. I got the paintings at my place."

Felipe hesitated, then said, "I can't. I gotta get back inside. I got chemistry next. That's important, chemistry."

Same old Felipe, thought Ramon. Gotta study! Gotta go to class! Doesn't he care about friends?

"Screw chemistry!" Ramon said. "What are you afraid of? Nobody cares if you go in there or not!"

"Well . . . *I* do," said Felipe as he turned to go into the building.

"Hey, Felipe," Ramon called after him. "You know what I think about guys that do nothing but study?"

Felipe turned back. "Probably the same that I think about guys that sell stolen paintings."

"Who's saying that! I didn't steal 'em," said Ramon, but by then Felipe was too far away to hear. "*I didn't steal 'em!*" Ramon shouted.

Felipe turned back and nodded. The nod meant: *OK, I believe you. Now let me go to class.*

Felipe Book-Eyes, thought Ramon. Maybe he's good in chemistry and hearts and lungs, but I bet I'm smarter than he is. 'Cause I don't believe all the shit people tell me about him! But he believes what they say about me!

Next time I see him, I'm gonna tell him that.

17

It was a bright October day. The path leading to the Central Park Zoo was thronged with people enjoying the crisp fall weather. Young and old in suits and dresses, in jeans and jogging outfits, walked, roller-skated, and bicycled by in an endless festive parade. I bet Glasser would really like this, thought Ramon. It's better than them trees he went crazy about. Maybe I'll bring him here, tomorrow. He could even help me sell his stuff.

Everywhere, vendors sold hot dogs and soda from carts with yellow-and-blue umbrellas, while street peddlers hawked necklaces and scarves from upturned crates, sold portable radios, wallets, belts, flowers, even poems on strips of pink and blue paper.

I could sell what I write like that, Ramon thought.

Maybe I will. 'Cause I ain't selling any paintings, that's for freaking sure. He adjusted the paintings once more on the park bench he'd taken over earlier.

He took a long drink from a can of raspberry soda, then called to the passersby again, "Here! Here! Check them out! Original paintings. Original! The great Arnold Glasser! The famous American painter whose stuff is in books and everything!"

After two hours, his voice was growing hoarse. People stopped and looked, but the only offer he'd gotten was for five dollars. Ramon had refused it.

Man, he thought, it just ain't no good here. I better go back to Fifth Avenue. They're selling too much junk here. Look at that guy there, with them handbags. He calls them leather, but they're plastic! All these weirdos going by, that's what they want, junk handbags! Junk bracelets! Junk belts! They don't know what good stuff is. They're all phony, so they buy phony stuff.

"Hey, hey, hey! Check 'em out! Quality paintings," Ramon called again.

A young couple in brightly colored outfits roller-skated toward Ramon. Their elbow pads and knee pads were red, matching their red helmets. They looked at the paintings while they steadied themselves on their skates.

"A street kid selling oil paintings," said the man, loudly. "Now I've seen everything! I've seen it all!"

125

Ramon spit some soda onto the ground. "No you ain't!" he called. "You ain't seen yourself in the mirror!"

"Hey look, you little four-letter-word, you—" the man began, but the woman with him cut in.

"Josh, come on! Don't let him get to you! He's ethnic minority; leave him alone."

"I guess you're right," said the man. "Let's go before I lose my cool."

So I'm ethnic minority, am I, thought Ramon. They say that like as if I'm a freak or something. I'm gonna get them!

As they turned to skate away, Ramon called after them, loud enough for everyone nearby to hear, "Hey! Hey! Everybody! Buy an ethnic *majority*! Five dollars each! The red-helmet special! The knee pads are free! Wind 'em up! Yeah! They talk! They walk! They skate!"

As he taunted them, Ramon's words fueled his anger, and his voice rose to a shout. The man skating away turned back for a moment as if to shout back, but thought better of it and skated on.

"Yeah! Yeah!" Ramon continued. "Five dollars each! Use their heads for piggy banks! You unscrew their ears, and you put your pennies in! Buy 'em! Buy 'em! Rattle your pennies inside their heads! You fill 'em up with pennies, you win a free trip to California!"

The roller-skaters were gone, but a policeman,

hearing the shouting, had walked over to Ramon's bench. Oh mama, here it comes, thought Ramon. I've had it.

"You got a permit to sell in the park?" the policeman asked.

"A what?"

"A permit. You got to have a permit."

"But nobody else . . . They ain't got permits," Ramon said, pointing to some of the vendors.

"Yes they have," said the policeman.

"You ain't checked them! How do you know! You ain't—"

"Hey look, kid," said the policeman, "I know them. They've got permits."

"No, they ain't. Down over there. I heard someone hustling pot. You telling me they got a permit for selling pot?"

"Kid, believe me, if I see it, I'll get them," the policeman said. "You been shouting here like a crazy guy, you know? I seen you here an hour ago; I didn't touch you; you were behaving yourself. OK, a kid playing hooky; it's a beautiful day. Who cares? But you make me notice you, that's different. I could get you for no permit, for truancy, for misuse of a park bench, and I think I see a knife bulging there in your right pocket. That could be a very serious offense. I could put you away for six months, easy. But you're just a kid. So all I'm telling you to do is walk out of the park. Get lost. Just take that junk you got there and walk out of the park. You heard me good, right, kid?"

"Yeah, but this stuff ain't junk. This is good stuff. By a famous painter," said Ramon.

"Sure, sure; I know. Great stuff. Now just—"

"You like 'em? Hey, you wanna buy one?" Ramon asked quickly.

"Kid, you take the cake! You really take the cake! Get that junk out of here, fast, before I forget you're only a kid. You got that?"

"Yeah . . ." said Ramon as he gathered the paintings together. "But they ain't junk!"

"Then why are you hustling them? Let them sell it in them Madison Avenue galleries."

"What galleries?"

"Madison Avenue. One block east, kid. Let *them* tell you if it's junk. Now beat it!"

Ramon's mind had jumped ahead of the policeman's words. That's good, he thought. Yeah! I could sell this stuff to an art gallery! They know all about this stuff. They'll know it's good! Hey, I'm gonna do it!

Ramon hefted the canvases under his arm, took a few steps, stopped, then went back to the bench to pick up his can of soda for one long final drink in defiance of the policeman.

"You're a real comedian, kid," said the policeman, taking out his black leather book, as if ready to write out a citation.

"Yeah. Thanks. So long," said Ramon as he walked briskly away. Then he turned for one last word. "Hey, do they pay you off in hot dogs or necklaces, man?"

The policeman started toward Ramon, but Ramon had already scrambled between two benches and was racing toward a low wall at the edge of the park. He held the paintings over his head like a tabletop, so he could run faster. When it became clear that he wasn't being chased, he slowed to a rapid walk. Hey, he thought, why do I do crazy stuff like that? I dunno. I guess 'cause I'm crazy. Like *papá*, when he hit that cop.

It took only a minute for Ramon to reach Madison Avenue. Antique shops, art galleries, and fine clothing stores lined both sides of the avenue. The shops and galleries seemed to Ramon like that hotel lobby he had once invaded, someone else's world, as unreal and untouchable as his television daydreams. Even the names of the galleries seemed forbidding: Kronmeyer Galleries, Larson and Danbury Fine English Furnishings, Lindemann Gallery, Doris Selig Ltd., Harmon and Holstein, Karl Jacobsen Fine Prints and Maps.

Ramon stood outside Harmon and Holstein, looking at the brightly colored pictures in huge gold frames. A small sign with block letters carried the names: *Klee, Miró, Chagall, Léger, Rouault, Mondrian.* I dunno, thought Ramon. They're just gonna throw me out. What's the use? But Glasser's pictures, they look like some of that stuff in the window. At least the colors do. . . . What the hell! Let 'em throw me out!

The gallery was white. Ceiling, walls, lamps, all were a soft white. The paintings on the walls, by contrast, seemed blinding with their raging colors. There was a stillness in the empty gallery; every step Ramon took clicked loudly on the parquet floor.

At a desk near the rear, a man in a light-gray suit half rose as Ramon walked slowly toward him.

"May I be of some help!" the man said firmly, half crouched at his desk as if ready to spring at the least provocation. His voice echoed off the walls.

"Yeah. I—you know—I got some paintings here," said Ramon nervously, hearing his voice resound in the bare room. "Like maybe they're good and you could buy them. You wanna look?"

"We don't buy paintings off the street," said the man with a sharp finality to his voice.

"They ain't off the street. They're by a good painter. Arnold Glasser. He's, like, a friend of mine."

"I'm very sorry. But we're not interested."

"Could you just *look* a minute?"

The man sighed with impatience. "I suppose I'll have to," he said. "Bring them back here."

Ramon took the paintings and leaned them against the wall near the man's desk. Then he stood aside, studying every change in the man's face for a sign of interest. The man looked at the paintings for a moment, but his face remained a smooth mask.

"Glasser . . . Glasser . . . The name sounds familiar. . . . Well," he said, "where did you get them?"

"Like I said, I got a friend. He painted them. His paintings are in a book—"

"How old is this friend?"

"I dunno. I think he said seventy-six."

"They look it."

"What d'ya mean?"

"That's right out of 1935. Low-level Shahn."

"Huh? . . . Hey, mister, I don't understand."

"Young man, you don't *have* to understand."

"Yes I do! He's my friend!"

The man sighed loudly. "All right. I'll enunciate clearly. Those paintings are derivative. They imitate other paintings. They're old-fashioned. If they were original old-fashioned that might be interesting, but they're unoriginal old-fashioned, and that's not interesting. Your friend might be a very nice gentleman, but we only handle the best of the best. . . . Don't look so crushed. The work isn't amateur. There is some merit in it. But not enough for us."

"Thanks," said Ramon softly.

Mister, thought Ramon, Glasser's worth ten of you. You got a face like an ice-skating rink. I could ice-skate on your face! I bet you never laughed in your whole freaking life.

Within the next hour, Ramon tried Lindemann Galleries, Doris Selig Ltd., the Altman Fine Arts Gallery, Van Buren Ltd., and Kronmeyer Galleries. Most of the gallery owners scarcely looked at the paintings, suggesting Ramon try somewhere else.

It ain't no use, he thought. I been in six, seven places and it ain't no use. The minute they see me, they've made up their freaking minds. You gotta have somebody dressed good to sell this stuff around here. You gotta have a grown-up who looks rich. And I don't know nobody who looks rich.

As he walked down Madison Avenue, Ramon hissed *bastardo* each time he passed a gallery. To hell with them all, he thought. Everybody takes care of themselves in New York. And I'm gonna take care of myself. . . . That reminds me. I better not meet Angel or any of them guys with all these paintings. Maybe I better go downtown on Madison all the way to Forty-fourth, then go across town that way. 'Cause they don't usually hang out down on Forty-fourth— Hey, wait . . . what's that?

In the window of Nielsen Galleries was a blue-and-red painting that looked like Glasser's. Ramon stopped and stared at the painting; it was signed Ben Shahn. The name seemed familiar. Something that first gallery owner had said. Something about Shawn or Shahn. Or Kahn. Ramon looked at the painting another moment, then decided to go in.

18

With its dark wood paneling and deep-red carpets, the Nielsen Galleries seemed majestically old. Yet many of the paintings were modern. Colors spun and slashed across the canvases; the frames seemed scarcely able to contain them.

Ramon saw a heavyset elderly man in a rear storage room busily sorting a collection of unframed paintings, leaning them one by one against a wall. He didn't seem to notice Ramon in the otherwise empty gallery.

Ramon glanced at the paintings and the little numbered cards next to them, identifying each work. Miró, Kandinsky, Braque, Picasso. Ramon knew Picasso. The card read: *No. 14, Pablo Picasso, Pipes, Tasse, Guitare, oil on canvas, 1911.* The painting was a strange blur of brown squares with musical scrolls and table edges worked into it.

Oh man, thought Ramon. Picasso's stuff is worth a lot. Glasser says so, and he oughta know. . . . I could steal that painting. Easy. I could stick it in with Glasser's. Yeah, and beat it the hell out of here fast. . . . I could do all kinds of stuff if I had the money from that painting. . . . I could get my *mamá* out of that shit hospital. Stuff like that. I oughta do it. . . . Yeah, I could show them guys in the gang who's macho! Just some brown paint and it's worth more than they'll ever rip off in their whole lives. . . . How could I sell it? I could figure it out. You read in the papers. There's ways. . . .

Ramon reached out toward the painting, just to touch it. Just to see . . . He pushed the painting sideways slightly, then let it come back to rest. There didn't seem to be any alarm attached to it.

He touched the frame again, then moved his fingers over the canvas. The dry paint felt rough, like clay pottery. He thought of Glasser in the museum, shouting at him to stop touching the painting of Columbus. He pulled his hand back. The painting's endless squares and cubes in shades of brown and yellow seemed like a dream of castles, chairs, tables, boxes, old boxes from Puerto Rico. Boxes full of pictures of his father as a child. Of his mother as a little girl all in white.

Ramon took a step back from the painting. I could never sell it, he thought. All I'd do is, I'd get everybody in New York out after me.

There was a voice behind him. "Well, I see you're quite an admirer of Picasso." Ramon spun around. The heavyset man stood with a small painting in his hand.

"Yeah. Yeah. I like Picasso a lot," said Ramon.

"And you're planning to buy one, right? Checking the frame, making sure the paint is dry?"

Ramon scurried in his mind for an answer. "Uh . . . I never seen a real painting by Picasso before. I dunno how he did that, with all them different layers. It's like when you drop a deck of cards. Like layers of brown cards, all over. Huh? . . ."

"Not bad. A dropped deck of cards. Imaginative. . . . By the way, I'm licensed to carry a gun. I'm so glad you weren't thinking about borrowing the painting . . . like the ones you're carrying. Hmm?"

"Hey yeah! That's why I came in! That one in the window is like my friend's. Arnold Glasser? He's a friend of mine and I'm trying to sell these to—"

"Well! A friend of yours, is he! Arnold Glasser happens to be dead. He's been dead for years."

"What! You're crazy, man! I seen him yesterday!"

"Oh really? What does he look like? And where is he?"

"He's . . . well he's pretty old. And he lives all alone by himself. He's in a wheelchair, you know, but his hands are strong. And he doesn't shave all the time. And he lives on West Eighty-fourth Street.

And he keeps saying his paintings stink."

The man thought for a moment, then, reaching a decision, said crisply, "Bring those paintings back to my office. Follow me." He walked quickly to the rear room, set the small painting down, then started riffling through a Manhattan phone book. "Glasser . . . Glasser . . ."

"He ain't got a phone," said Ramon.

"So I see. . . . No Arnold Glasser in the book. . . . Hmm . . . Well! Let's see the paintings."

"Yeah! OK!" Ramon spread the paintings out against the wall, then stood to one side.

The man nodded. "That's Glasser all right. Hasn't changed his style in forty years. Whom did he remind you of, in the window? Shahn?"

"Yeah, that's the one, man!"

"A small correction. My name isn't *man;* it's Nielsen. . . . So you saw the resemblance to Ben Shahn. Very acute of you. Glasser was one of them. One of the WPA painters. Only Glasser never caught on. Never really made it. . . ."

"Yeah? How come?"

"Hard to tell. Bad luck? Narrow range? Or most likely, too much nose thumbing at everyone. He didn't give a damn. Admirable in a way. . . . Is he really alive?"

"Yeah! We went to the Museum of Art a couple of days ago."

"Well I'll be damned. I thought he was dead. I

136

knew him back in the forties. In fact, I reviewed his work; I used to do art criticism for the *Times*. He was already in a decline then. . . . I suppose my art reviews didn't help. No, they weren't too kind. One regrets with hindsight. . . . Well, well. . . . I wonder if I ought to try to have lunch with him. Could be painful for both of us, though. Mmm . . . It would be nice to see him, in a way. . . ."

"Yeah? Why don't you sell his stuff? Then you could pay him in person, man— I mean Nielsen."

"Impossible. And it's *Mr.* Nielsen. . . . Say, what's *your* name, anyway?"

"Ramon. If his stuff's good, why can't you try to sell it? You got that Shahn guy there."

"Ben Shahn was one of the greatest artists America has ever—"

"Yeah," Ramon cut in, "but Glasser, he needs it more."

"True enough. True enough. But I can't. We're running an art gallery, not a charity."

"Hey come on, Mr. Nielsen. Look at that wall," said Ramon, pointing to a blank wall. "You could put all his stuff up on that wall and still have room to play handball. Come on. Give us a break."

"Us?"

"Yeah. I'm Glasser's, what do you call— his agent. Come on, just take three of 'em. Maybe somebody'll buy one. Huh? Mr. Nielsen?"

"No. Impossible . . . Of course, there's some renewed interest in the 1930's artists, I must admit."

"Yeah! Mr. Nielsen! Please?"

"I'd have to sign contracts with him. It's too messy."

"Naa, I'm his agent. We don't need contracts. Mr. Nielsen, please?"

"Young man, if I sold one of these for a thousand—"

"Oh mama! A thousand dollars!"

"He could sue me for *fifty* thousand. We have to have agreements—"

"OK! OK! You take these paintings—and you put 'em on the wall. But don't sell 'em yet. Then I'll get Glasser over here. But I won't tell him what's happening. I wanna surprise him. Then when he gets here, he'll sign everything. OK? Mister? OK?"

"How do I know he'll sign everything?"

"I'm his agent! Don't worry. OK? Huh?"

"Surprise him, eh? Hmm . . ."

"Yeah. Please? Mr. Nielsen, please?"

"Well . . . I don't want you to think I'm doing this because of the past. I'm not! But . . . there really is some renewed interest in that generation of artists. There could be money here. Hmm . . . Surprise him, eh? Old Glasser. Hmmm . . . Well. Glasser has a good agent. You may have a future there, young man. Ramon. How old are you, anyway?"

"Fourteen."

"You look twelve."

"Thanks!"

"That's not an insult. Or maybe it is, at your age. I wouldn't mind looking twelve. And I wouldn't mind looking as thin as you, either. . . . So you're only fourteen, eh? Where did you get all your street smarts?"

"From the street," said Ramon with a smirk.

"Uh-huh. I see I have a wise guy on my hands."

"Hey! That's what Glasser keeps calling me!"

"It takes one to know one . . . All right. Leave the paintings with me and I'll put them in temporary frames. We'll have them up . . . today's Monday. Come over with Glasser Wednesday morning."

"Yeah, OK!"

"You're the youngest individual I've ever had to deal with," said Nielsen as he gathered the paintings together. "But certainly not the dumbest, by far. Now I think you'd better go, before I change my mind. And keep your hands off the Picasso as you leave."

"Hey! Don't change your mind! I'm going! Thanks! I'm going! So long!"

Ramon tried not to show any emotion as he walked out of the gallery. But once on the street a safe distance away, he drummed on a metal mailbox and shouted, *"Yah-hoo!"*

Bueno, bueno, he thought. Is Glasser gonna be glad he met me! I got him a real gallery! I did it! Me! All alone! I did it!

19

It was Dopey Luis again. Ramon spotted him in the deepening shadows of the buildings, as he turned the corner at Eighty-fourth Street. Dopey Luis continued to ride his bike loaded with groceries up Columbus Avenue.

Maybe he didn't even see me, thought Ramon. Maybe he's just working. I don't care. I'm going up to Glasser's whether he seen me or not. Them guys ain't gonna scare me out.

Wait'll I tell them how much money this gallery can get for one of Glasser's paintings. And they're still getting half my cut! Those dumb freaks! I'm making more money for them with this than they could rip off in six months. Harpo, he'd never be able to do this. Or Angel. Or any of them. 'Cause it takes style. And brains. And they ain't got neither.

As Dopey Luis continued up the next block, he looked back quickly toward Ramon, then rode on.

He seen me all right. OK! I ain't taking any more of this shit! I'm gonna find Harpo and talk to him tomorrow. Or maybe I'll find him tonight. I'll just go up and tell Glasser about Wednesday, so he's ready for the big surprise, and then I'm gonna lay it all out for Harpo. They better quit following me!

At Glasser's apartment, Ramon waited for the usual unlocking of bolts and chains. He remembered the first time he'd been there, hand on his knife, trying to pretend he was calm. Trying to be as cool as Harpo.

Harpo. That freak. Harpo would have killed Glasser on the spot if it had been him.

The door opened and Ramon saw Glasser in his wheelchair, unshaven, his hair in disarray, his shirt half open. In his lap was the book he'd shown to Ramon: *Despair and Hope: The Painters of the 1930's.*

"So," said Glasser very softly. "So . . . Come in . . . if you want. . . ." His eyes looked like the eyes in that Rembrandt painting, tired and defeated.

"Yeah, I wanna come in," said Ramon. "Why d'ya think I'm here?"

"So then come in. . . ."

Glasser wheeled back to the living room, silently, taking no notice of Ramon. The living room was dim and gloomy; Glasser hadn't turned on any lights.

Ramon wondered how Glasser could see the pictures in that book. "Hey, Glasser, have they turned your power off, too?"

Glasser didn't seem to hear. "Hmm?" he murmured.

Ramon went to the light switch and turned on the lights.

"Turn that off!" called Glasser. "I want it dark!"

"Come on, Glasser! I can't talk to you in the dark," said Ramon.

"I can hear you just as well in the dark. Better!" Glasser wheeled over to the switch and turned the lights off.

He's crazy again, thought Ramon. Next thing, he'll be asking me to kill him or something, just like before.

"Hey Glasser. I got a surprise for you, OK?"

"Hmm . . ."

"This Wednesday we gotta go someplace. Only I can't tell you where or anything. 'Cause it's a surprise."

"What surprise?" Glasser murmured.

"I can't tell you. Yet!"

"I've had enough surprises in my life. I don't need any more, thank you just the same," said Glasser in a low voice.

"But this one's a good one!"

"Hmm . . ."

"You're beautiful! What a downer!" said Ramon. "I come all the way across town just to tell you about this surprise, and all you do is sit there in the dark."

Glasser didn't answer. In the darkness, his figure seemed hunched in the wheelchair as if he were trying to disappear. Ramon turned the light on again. Glasser remained in the same position in the wheelchair, staring vacantly at the book in his lap.

"Hey, you been looking at that book?" asked Ramon. " 'Cause you can't see anything in the dark."

"I know what's in this book," Glasser said softly. "I don't have to see it. A dead man named A. Glasser is in this book. Now turn off the light."

"No! Next thing, you'll be telling me to knife you again!"

"Good idea."

Ramon wondered if he should tell Glasser everything about the Nielsen Galleries. Would that help?

"Hey, Glasser. I could tell you about Wednesday. I could tell you about this surprise, OK? I don't wanna, but I could. Because if I tell you, you'll be happy. But I don't wanna tell you, 'cause I never had anything like this in my whole life, this thing that's gonna happen on Wednesday. OK? Can't you just get happy if I promise you, I swear, that this surprise'll make you feel good?"

Glasser sighed and looked up at Ramon. Then he nodded several times. "All right . . . All right . . . I think too much sometimes, that's all. . . . Being old and a flop isn't much fun. . . ."

Ramon grabbed the book from Glasser's lap and held it up. "Hey Glasser! I ain't in a book like this! Nobody I know is! Except you! So if you're a flop, then I'm total shit! 'Cause I'm *never* gonna get in a book like this in my whole freaking life, and I know it!"

"Don't be so sure. . . . Fourteen, and he knows it!" Glasser turned his wheelchair and pointed toward the wall. "Look! Know-it-all! You already have a fan. Me!" Hanging on the wall, enclosed in an oversized frame, was the sheet Ramon had ripped from his notebook and given to Glasser.

"You put that on the wall? How come?" Ramon walked over and looked at the words he'd written.

"Why not?" said Glasser. "It's a work of art, too."

"But it ain't no good."

"I like it."

"Yeah? My *mamá* used to put pictures I made in school up on the wall, too."

"I'm not your mother! I've read enough books in my time," said Glasser with a sweep of his arm toward his bookshelves. "I hope to think I know what's good and what isn't. I don't put just any old thing on my living-room walls. These walls are my last fortress, mister! Only the best goes up."

"Well that thing I wrote ain't so good. . . . I wrote better stuff than that. . . ."

"Good. Prove it."

Ramon hesitated, then took the notebook out of his pocket. He looked at it a moment, shrugged, then tossed it into Glasser's lap.

Glasser picked up the book and thumbed through it, reading sentences at random. He paused, reread a sentence, then read it aloud, " 'Saturday, October sixth. Glasser got these curtains. They make a shadow like a leopard, walking smooth.' It should be smoothly, but not when it's poetry like this. Smooth is right. . . . OK, Ramon Santiago! No more baloney! You can't spell. Your grammar is terrible. But I think you've got something! You should write and then write more. Do you hear me?"

"Yeah. That's why I got that book."

"Good. Fill it. Then get another. And another. If something hurts, write it. If it makes you angry, write it. You see? So you can tell people what it's like to be you. To live where you live with a door half made of air. That's your knife, that book. Do you understand?"

"Yeah . . . I dunno . . . You really think I can write good? Don't shit me!"

"I said you can. With a lot of work, college, everything—and maybe a little luck—you could become what I didn't."

"College? Me?"

"Yes, yes! Of course, you!"

"Naa. I dunno . . . There's a guy I know who wants to go to college. But everybody, they think he's weird. *I* don't, but they do. Felipe Book-Eyes, they call him. Nobody goes near him, 'cause they think he's weird."

"Good! Be weird! Which means be yourself. I may not be King of the Mountain, I may not even be Duke of the Dump Heap, but I'm *me*! Yes? Right? Yes or no?"

"Yeah. Yeah, you sure are. . . ."

"Good. My speech is finished. You've cheered me up, with your leopards walking smooth. In fact, you've cheered me up, period. Why are you standing there like an idiot with my book? Here's *your* book back, give me *my* book back, and let's make dinner. This time, *I'm* hungry!"

"Naa. I gotta get back downtown. I gotta see some guys about something. You know, business."

"Aha. The surprise?"

"Oh, uh, sort of. Yeah."

"So . . . come on over whenever you like."

"OK. Wednesday morning, right?"

"Wait a minute!" said Glasser. "What about school Wednesday morning?"

"No classes Wednesday morning," Ramon said quickly. "So be ready, Glasser. And shave!"

"All right! All right! That's all I need! A fourteen-year-old *nudzh*!"

"What's that?"

"A *nudzh* is someone who keeps telling you to shave every half hour."

146

"What about someone who keeps telling you to go to school every ten minutes?"

"That's a wise elderly adviser."

"Hey! You finally admitted you're elderly! So long, *Señor* Arbotsky *Viejo*."

"So long, *Señor Nudzh!*"

20

Ramon walked slowly toward home along Columbus Avenue, trying to remember exactly what Glasser had said about his writing. *You've got something. You should write. And then write more. If something hurts, write it.* He touched his knife, then he touched the book in his other pocket.

That book was his knife, Glasser had said. But he needed his knife. Only Felipe could get away without carrying a knife. Was he really like Felipe? No! The gang wanted him to join them! They would never ask Felipe! . . . But what was so wrong with being like Felipe?

Ramon was close to his neighborhood, to Harpo's territory, but he wanted to think some more about what Glasser had said. About Felipe. About everything. He could find Harpo later.

He headed for his secret place in the old railroad cut on Fifty-third Street. As he scrambled and skidded down the embankment toward his spot among the tires and weeds, he pushed against the hulk of an old boiler to stop his slide. The metal felt cool in the October evening.

Crouched in his spot, low on the ground, he wondered if he looked like another gray tire from above. Another gray person, like millions of others. *A talent. A gift.* Maybe he was more than another gray person. Maybe. Maybe. He pulled out his book, found a clean page, and quickly wrote:

October 8.
Got my book in my left pocket, knife in the other.
Book is my sister, knife is my brother. I need them
both.

Hey, that ain't bad, thought Ramon. Maybe I'll show it to Glasser. I need them both. Yeah, I do.

There was a sound of gravel grinding against gravel from above. Ramon looked up.

At the break in the fence, squeezing through one at a time, were Harpo, Dopey Luis, Angel, and Julio. They began scrambling and sliding down the embankment, one after the other.

Oh man. I'm dead. I'm dead. I can't take 'em all on. And I can't get past them. Think! Think! Talk to 'em! Talk!

"Hey, Harpo!" called Ramon, standing up, his

hand in his knife pocket. "*Amigo!* I been looking for you! Where you been?"

They had reached the bottom; they stood in a line in front of him.

"You been looking for me! You little shit!" There was a knife in Harpo's hand now, and the others, following his lead, took out their knives, also. Ramon's hand gripped his knife, but he didn't pull it out.

No use. No use. Four against one. I gotta talk.

"Hey, come on, Harpo. I told Angel, right? I told him any money I make, you guys get half. I told him. And I gave him forty bucks, right?"

"You shit! You joined them. The ones who spit on us! You wanna be one of them! *Maricón! Bastardo!*"

"Hey, man, I ain't one of them. I'm with you. I *am!*"

"You push that guy's wheelchair all over the freaking city! You're with us my ass, man!"

"But he's OK! He don't spit on me! He's my friend. My *friend!*"

"Let's get this freak!"

In the blur of bodies, Ramon leaped sideways. The knife was out now, a steel claw in his fist. He moved behind a junked refrigerator lying on its side with its door opened downward like a gaping metal mouth. Harpo and the others froze for a second.

"Spread out! Spread out!" called Harpo. "Get behind the little freak!"

Oh man, I can't get out of it! Oh mama! Oh mama! I gotta get Harpo. Harpo and Angel. Luis and Julio, they're scared. It's Harpo and Angel I gotta get.

Ramon leaped over the refrigerator and made a feint toward Harpo, his knife out at arm's length. Harpo backed away. They circled a quarter of a circle.

There was a scrape of gravel to his left. Ramon pivoted; Angel backed off.

"Hey. Four on one! Come on! *Basta ya!* Give me a break! Come on!"

"Shove it, man!"

The back of Ramon's neck prickled with sudden electric feeling. Behind him! He swung around fast; Dopey Luis scrambled away. They were afraid of him all right. Good! Good! He whirled back. Harpo had tried to move in.

Then the flurry of an arm to his left; Ramon swung his knife and stabbed, but it was too late. His left shoulder felt as if a sharp sliver of ice had gone in and melted. There was blood sliding down his chest; on his shirt a red stain grew and spread.

I gotta get past. I gotta! Ramon leaped toward Angel and his knife flicked. There was a crease of blood along Angel's arm. Ramon whirled back toward Harpo, but it was too late. Julio had tackled him from one side, while Harpo's knife darted forward. The knife blade went in and out of Ramon's neck in the instant before he fell. His head slammed against the metal door of the open refrigerator.

Ramon heard blurred voices above him. "Hey man . . . hey . . . you killed him. . . . Shit, let's . . . hey, let's get . . . hell out of here. . . . You killed him. . . . He's OK. . . . No . . . look at all . . . blood. . . . He got *me*. . . . Only wanted to cut him a little. . . . He's dead. . . . Let's get outa here. . . ."

Then silence. Sounds of grinding gravel at the embankment. Silence again. They were gone. Ramon pressed his hand against his neck. His neck and chest were slick with blood.

Oh mama. Oh mama. I'm bleeding to death. Gotta get outa here. Get out. Get out.

He felt for his knife on the ground, but it was gone. With his hand pressed to his neck, Ramon struggled toward the embankment and grappled his way up, sliding on the gravel, recovering, pulling himself up on pieces of discarded junk. On Fifty-third Street he started running east toward Tenth Avenue, toward Broadway, toward people. He pushed against his neck but the blood kept coming.

He ran wildly, not quite sure where he was heading. He heard a buzzing in his ears and his legs felt wooden, as if they were attached to someone else. He couldn't run; he only thought he was running. His legs wouldn't move, yet he had to keep going. He knelt down, trying to crawl.

"Oh mama. Oh mama," he mumbled. Blood from his neck and shoulder had formed a trail along the sidewalk. He fell sideways to the pavement.

A voice. A woman. "Call the police! He's been stabbed! Police! Call the police!"

The buzzing in his ears grew to a white roar. The pavement against his face felt rough but comforting. He pressed against the pavement, knowing he couldn't fall any farther.

The woman's voice blurred with the roar in his ears. Everything had become a dream. Above him, in slow motion, a policeman asked questions. Ramon answered, but his tongue felt thick. Someone else's tongue. *I dunno. I dunno who did it. . . . They got my watch. I dunno who did it. . . . I dunno. I dunno.*

Then, in a blur, the pavement seemed to lift, seemed to be a bed taking him away, moving, with a siren above his head. EEE-AWW! EEE-AWW! EEE-AWW!

The donkey sound loud above his head.

21

As they carried him from the ambulance to the long white table in the emergency room, Ramon felt strangely as if he were on the roller coaster at Coney Island.

"I'm OK . . . I'm OK . . . I can walk . . ." he mumbled.

"Relax, kid. Relax. You got a free vacation. Enjoy it," said a white-coated man.

On the table in the emergency room, things started to blur again. A nurse asked questions just as the policeman had. He thought he'd answered them but she asked again: his name, his address, his phone, where were his parents, what apartment, what hospital, what prison, what social worker, what age, what religion, his name, his address, his phone . . .

Everything blurred again. He lay on the long white

table and saw, in a yellow haze, two lights on the ceiling moving slowly into focus and joining to become one. There was a green shade around the light, a green magic halo that could make the single light spread to two, then move together again.

"I'm OK. I can walk," he said weakly.

"Not yet, kid," said a man to his left.

Ramon let his eyes focus downward. There was a doctor in a light-green hospital coat and a nurse with a blurred face and blurred red hair.

"This is going to hurt. Ready?"

The sharp thin pain of a needle moved through his neck.

"One more."

Again the pain, a few inches from the first. Ramon ground his teeth and stared at the ceiling light's green rim. Green grass, he thought as the needle slid in. Think of green! Green hat! Green sky! Green sun!

His neck felt numb. The doctor's fingers touched him, but Ramon felt only a dense cool pressure.

"There. That doesn't hurt anymore, right?"

"Yeah."

"You're lucky you're alive, kid. Half an inch to the left—finished! Missed the jugular by *that* much . . ."

He felt metal touching and pushing, but no pain, only numbness. His head moved slightly as the doctor worked on his neck.

"OK, we can start the stitches. We'll get the shoulder later, kid. The shoulder's nothing. . . . How did it happen?"

"My watch," said Ramon. "These two guys, they got my watch . . . you know? . . . I tried to get away, so they cut me. . . ."

"Is that what you told the police?"

"Yeah . . . it's the truth, man . . ." said Ramon, weakly.

"Oh, I believe it, kid," said the doctor. "But you sure look like you've been in a gang fight. . . ."

"No! I had . . . I had this gold watch. Fake gold. But it looked real . . ."

"OK, stop moving your head. . . . You're going to look nice after this. Fifteen stitches, maybe more, in the neck. Eight or nine in the shoulder. You'll look like Frankenstein's monster. You ever see that movie, kid?"

"Yeah. On TV."

Ramon's thoughts came more quickly now. Glasser. What would Glasser think? Wednesday! Would he be able to take Glasser to the Nielsen Galleries?

"Hey, uh . . . how long am I, like, gonna have to stay in the hospital?"

"Kid, when we get you sewn up, you sit for half an hour and then you walk out of here. If you want to stay here, you better get your friends to aim better."

"They ain't no friends!"

"Kid, I don't care. Tell it to the police. . . . Hold still!"

"Is this Westside Hospital?" asked Ramon, hoping the doctor would stop asking about his fight.

"You bet it is. Can't you hear the paint peeling?"

"My *mamá*, she's in this hospital," said Ramon.

"Oh yes? How nice. She belong to a gang, too?"

"I don't belong to no gang!"

"OK, OK! Hold still, kid. Last stitch . . . OK. There. Your neck is done! Let's do the shoulder."

The sharp, thin needle probed again, and then numbness. The doctor hummed slightly out of tune as he worked. In a few minutes he pressed hard against Ramon's shoulder. "There! Last stitch," he said. "Beautiful. The girls will love you. You have a girl friend, kid?"

"Naa . . . but I will."

"Well, you'll look nice and tough for her. You can brag about how you got your scars, after the bandages come off. We're going to tape you up. The girls will love that, too. You'll be a big-shot hero in the *barrio*."

"Hey, you know?" said Ramon. "How come all you doctors don't cut each other up? You could do it very sanitary. Then you could stitch each other up. And then all the girls would love it, too. Then *you* could be a big hero. In the hospital."

The doctor stopped working; his face loomed above Ramon, blocking out the ceiling light. "Hey look, I don't need your lip! I'm sewing you up here, for free. You don't have to pay a cent; and you give me lip! You got nerve, kid."

"Yeah. Well some guys don't like that 'hero in the *barrio*' stuff too much. I know a guy, he cuts off rats' heads just for fun. You say that to him, he'd cut you up real good!"

"Is *that* what's bothering you? What I said about being a big hero in the *barrio*!"

"Yeah."

"Oh. I thought it was kind of funny. There's no telling taste."

"Yeah. 'Specially doctors'!"

"What's that?" asked the doctor.

"Nothing. I always thought doctors, like, they were something special, that's all."

"They are. You try working in this place for a month, and you'll find out it . . . OK. You can sit up."

Ramon sat up on the table, and the room spun around.

"Oh man, I'm dizzy."

"You will be for a while. You lost a lot of blood. I'll get a nurse to help you—"

"No! I can do it myself!"

Ramon slid off the table, then took hold of the edge. His legs felt shaky.

"Where . . . where do I go?"

"Out to the waiting room. Take this green card and give it to the nurse at the desk. Then sit for half an hour. If you feel faint, tell the nurse. Now listen. Don't take the bandages off. Don't get them wet. Sleep on your back. It'll hurt for a day or two. If it does, take two aspirins every four hours. Come back in ten days, and we'll take out the stitches. That's it. Keep up the good knife work, kid, and we'll do your face next time. Or maybe an ear."

Was that another insult? Ramon wondered as he walked to the waiting room. It probably was, but he felt too weak to get angry.

Ramon handed the green card to the nurse at the desk, but instead of sitting, he went to the elevator and pressed 7. At the door to his mother's room, he felt dizzy again. He held on to the door for a moment, took a deep breath, then walked in.

His mother was facing the window, but Ramon could see that there were no tubes attached to her. And at the side of the bed was a tray with some half-eaten food and an empty milk container. She's better, thought Ramon. She's eating again!

He bent over to see her, but suddenly his neck burned. I can't bend my neck! Thanks a lot, Harpo! Thanks a lot, Angel! You bastards!

Ramon felt his shirt. It was stiff with caked blood. If she sees all this blood and all these bandages, he thought, she'll get sick all over again. I better find something to cover my shirt.

He took a large white towel from a table and draped it around his neck and chest. Then he went back to the bed.

"Mami," he said softly. *"Soy yo."* His mother

struggled in the bed to turn toward him. "You don't have to move," Ramon said in Spanish. "I'll come over to your side." He walked around to the window.

"Ramon, is it you?" his mother asked weakly, in Spanish. She was better! She knew him!

"Sure, sure. It's me, Ramon. Hey, you've been eating. That's good!" he said in Spanish. He wished he could talk to her in English; it was a struggle sometimes to find the right words in Spanish.

"Yes . . . Yes, I ate a little . . ." his mother murmured.

"You've got to eat a lot! Come on! You've got to get a little bit fat, like you used to be."

His mother chuckled softly, then started coughing.

"Hey, take it easy," Ramon said.

She struggled to speak through her cough. "I . . . I was never fat. . . ."

"A little. But it's all right. That's the way I like you to be. Fat."

His mother laughed again. "Always fresh," she whispered. She studied Ramon silently for a moment. "You . . . you look sick. . . ."

"Who, me!" said Ramon. "I'm great. You're the one who's sick."

"You eat . . . good food . . . no junk . . . and clean the house," she said, just above a whisper.

"Sure, sure. Don't worry," he answered.

She stared at Ramon again, then gestured slightly toward the towel over his chest. "Why do you wear . . . that thing?"

"Oh. That's for sanitation. You've got to be, you know, sanitary to visit here."

"I'm tired," his mother said weakly. "I want to sleep. . . . Thank you, Ramon, for coming to visit me. . . ."

"Mami! You don't have to thank me! Shit, I'm your son!"

"No cursing. . . ."

"Right, right."

"Your mouth . . . is a pigpen."

"Come on! You should hear everybody else. . . . I'll be back soon, all right? Keep eating."

"Yes. . . . That picture . . ." She nodded toward Glasser's painting.

"Do you like it?"

"It's crazy. . . . There are no trees like that in the whole world. No place. . . . I'm tired . . . tired. . . ."

"Go back to sleep," said Ramon. "And keep eating. Eat a lot."

"Ramon . . . clean the house . . . and your mouth. . . ."

"Right, right, right. . . . Sleep good, OK?"

Ramon arranged her blanket, straightened Glasser's painting, and left. In the hallway he felt faint again. I feel lousy, he thought. But at least she's better. I even got her to laugh. . . .

The cool night air made his legs feel stronger. He stopped for a hot dog, keeping his hand spread over his bloody shirt, then walked slowly toward

Fifty-third Street and Eleventh Avenue. I gotta get my knife, he thought. It's down there by the train tracks someplace. Nobody's gonna get my knife but me.

At the railroad cut, he looked down for a minute to make sure no one was below. Then he slid down slowly, trying not to move his neck. His shoulder had started to hurt, also. I'm a cripple, he thought. Thanks, thanks, you bastards!

He searched the ground near the junked refrigerator. In the dim glow from the streetlight far above, he saw a dark patch of blood on the open door. My blood, he thought.

Near the refrigerator door, he saw the silver edge of his knife. He picked it up and examined the blade; the tip was dark with dry blood. Angel, he thought. That's Angel. Ramon closed the knife and dropped it into his right pocket. Then he took out his book and pencil, thumbed to a blank page, and wrote without looking down:

Ramon Santiago owes Harpo and Angel and Luis and Julio. The first one I meet, I cut.

22

His neck and shoulder ached all night. Ramon searched for aspirins in the dark bathroom. I gotta pay them bills, he thought. I gotta get that electricity turned on. Oh man, it hurts. . . . Maybe Mrs. Garcia got aspirins. . . . Naa! If I ask her for help, she'll never let go of me. . . . I'm just gonna think it don't hurt, then it *won't* hurt.

He slept badly, turning again and again, trying to find positions that didn't strain his neck or shoulder. He awoke at dawn and, dazed with loss of blood and lack of sleep, feverishly decided he had to clean the apartment. Keep the place clean, she said. Maybe she's coming home soon. 'Cause she's better. I gotta clean all this shit up. That refrigerator. Gotta throw the spoiled stuff out.

Though his neck and shoulder still ached, he

163

cleaned for hours, wrapping food in old newspapers, washing the empty refrigerator, then the kitchen linoleum. Exhausted and weak, he fell back into bed and slept till noon.

He awoke feeling stronger, but hungry. Oh man, I'm starving again. Glasser, he's right. I'm always hungry. He was still wearing his blood-drenched shirt. Ramon took it off slowly, maneuvering his arms carefully out of the sleeve, trying not to stretch the injured shoulder. He looked at his blood-caked shirt and thought of hanging it on the wall above his bed, next to Glasser's painting. That would be crazy, he decided. He wrapped the shirt in an old newspaper and threw it into the garbage.

He wondered whether he should go uptown and visit Glasser. No, it would be better to wait till tomorrow, till the Nielsen Galleries surprise. He had other business today. Today was Harpo Day. And Angel Day.

I'm gonna get one of them. My right arm is good. I can move just as good as always. I'll get some hot dogs or *empanadas* or something, then I'm gonna find them.

He stood in front of the mirror, turned away slowly, then spun around. "*Cuidado*! Look out!" The knife was in his hand, though his neck ached.

I'm gonna get them. I don't care if it hurts. I'm gonna get them.

He checked the hallway to make sure no one was

there, particularly Mrs. Garcia. If Mrs. Garcia saw his bandaged neck, she would follow him to the ends of the earth to find out what had happened.

On the street he headed for a fast-food restaurant. He ate hot dogs and drank *naranjada*, a sweet orangeade, from a narrow bottle. Deciding he was still hungry, he went across the street and bought another hot dog, then walked toward Tenth Avenue, looking for Harpo.

Hey Harpo, baby, he murmured to himself. I'm here, man! I ain't dead! Come on, Harpo, baby, let's play one on one. Let's see what you can do with your knife one on one.

He walked up Tenth Avenue to Sixtieth Street, then came back down Ninth. Nobody around, he thought. Yeah, they're cooling it good. They're smart. Or maybe they're just chicken. . . . Them and their macho. All they use it for is ripping off old ladies. And for four against one. That ain't macho. That's shit. . . .

Ramon searched for another hour, then returned to his apartment. He washed his face and, feeling tired again, slept till early evening.

He awoke, went out for more hot dogs, then strolled over to the huge parking lot near his house. He sat on the asphalt among a group of young people listening to New York-style Latin music blaring from three huge portable radios all playing together.

"Hey, good *salsa*," someone said to Ramon.

"Yeah, yeah," Ramon answered.

"Good loud boxes, hey?"

"Yeah, yeah, yeah."

"What've you got on your neck, man? Why've you got all that tape?"

"Oh. I, uh, got stung by a bee," said Ramon.

"How come you need all that tape for a bee? That musta been some bee!"

"Oh yeah, it was big. In Central Park, they're big. And, you know, it was like a whole swarm. Got it in my shoulder, too. Look!"

"Hey man! Them bees don't like you."

"Yeah," said Ramon.

"Good *salsa*, hey?"

"Yeah. My father, he likes it a lot."

"Tell him to come on out. Old guys, they can listen, too. We don't care. Tell him to come over."

"Naa. He's busy."

Ramon sat in the cool October night and let the Latin beat flow through him, trying to move his shoulders to the rhythm, even though his left shoulder still ached. The music made him think of his father somewhere far away in that brick-and-iron building. Alone. Could he listen to music there? His father, who loved music, was without music now. And his mother, who always sang—while she worked, while she cooked . . .

No more music. He couldn't listen anymore. The music hurt too much. The music, his shoulder, his neck, his thoughts. Everything hurt. He stood abruptly and headed toward home, walking between groups of teenagers huddled around their radios as if for warmth.

In bed, trying to fall asleep, Ramon thought about Glasser and the Nielsen Galleries again. His mood lifted. Tomorrow was going to be great! He took out his book and quickly wrote:

October 9.
Hey! Hey! Tomorrow is Glasser Day! Look out, New York City! We're coming!

Then he turned over on his good shoulder and fell asleep, the book still in his hand.

23

Ramon tried to fix his collar one last time, as the bolts clicked open on Glasser's door. It was hopeless. No matter how much he tugged at his shirt, the bandage still showed.

Glasser spotted the white tape on Ramon's neck as soon as he opened the door. "What happened to your neck?" he asked. "Is that your surprise?"

"You shaved!" said Ramon, trying to change the subject. "And you got your good brown sweater on! Hey, that's great."

"Hmm . . . So what happened to your neck?" Glasser asked as he wheeled toward the living room.

"Oh, nothing much. Some guys mugged me, that's all."

"Some guys? Which some guys?"

"I dunno."

"How about a delivery boy from Hansen's Market, as a wild guess! *My* delivery boy who hasn't come around lately!"

"Naa . . . I don't know who you mean. . . ."

Glasser wheeled directly in front of Ramon and glared at him. "I think you better get this clear, mister! If we're going to be associated in any way, business partners, friends, adviser-to-youth and youth-to-be-advised, there's one thing I won't take. That's dishonesty. You hear! I spent my life being honest and that's what I expect from my associates, few though they may be. If you're going to lie, or create Ramon Santiago fairy tales, then please go!"

Ramon sighed and sat down on the couch, while Glasser leaned back in his wheelchair. For a long moment they stared at one another.

"If you tell the cops, I'm dead," said Ramon very quietly.

"I'm your friend, not an informer," said Glasser.

"Yeah, they got me, the gang. Two nights ago. They cut me up good. My shoulder and my neck."

"Why?"

"I dunno. . . . They don't like what I'm doing. . . ."

"What you're doing? . . . You mean with me?"

"Yeah."

Glasser slumped slightly in his chair and wiped his face with his hand. "I should have known," he said. "That delivery boy followed us into the park the other day. Yes, I saw him. I should have known. I thought he was after me, but he was after you. . . . He's the one who said I had money, right? Who set up the whole thing?"

"Yeah."

"My grocery boy! Some city this is becoming. . . . It's insane! A boy sets me up to be robbed. Then he knifes you. And he's getting away scot-free!"

"Yeah."

"Why don't you tell the police? That kid tried to kill you!"

"Naa. They weren't gonna kill me. Just cut me up."

"It's an assault with a deadly weapon! You *have* to tell the police!"

"I don't have to do nothing!"

"They'll do it again!"

"No they won't. They got what they want. It's me that's gonna do something! I'm gonna get them!"

"*You're* going to get them! You stupid— That grocery boy! He's a foot taller than you!"

"I can handle him. One on one. The other night, it was four against one! But not anymore. I'll take them out one at a time."

"Go to the police. Stop trying to be the big hero!"

"I can't! Those guys'd get me! I won't be able to live there no more. Don't you know nothing!"

"Do you mean to tell me you can knife one of them, they can knife you, and nobody tells the police?"

"The knife stuff, that's between us. But the police! They're the enemy. That's why they knifed me. Because you, they think you're the enemy, too."

Glasser gestured as if to ask a question, then sat silently. After a moment he asked, "Then why . . . If they're ready to knife you for it, why do you come here?"

" 'Cause I feel like, that's all. I like coming here. You're my friend, right? They ain't gonna tell *me* what to do! Them freaks!"

"But at least you can forget about getting even. You said they'd leave you alone, didn't you? So put away that knife of yours and stop being so—"

"I need my knife! I need it! You know, you're, like, trying to make me into you!" Ramon shouted. "Well I ain't you! If I get cut by somebody I know, I don't call the cops! That's *your* style. What I do is I get even. That's *my* style! And that's the way it is!"

"I don't believe in this your style, my style business," said Glasser. "I don't believe it! We're all human! That's the only style! Do you understand what I'm saying? Yes or no?"

"Yeah! Yeah! I understand! OK?"

"Good. Now it's up to you. Enough! Finished! . . . All right. Let's get to your surprise."

"Yeah. We gotta move it! It's getting late."

It was a perfect morning for the park, but Ramon scarcely noticed. As he pushed the wheelchair along the winding path toward the East Side and the Nielsen Galleries, he tried to answer Glasser's arguments again, in his own mind.

I know what the guy's trying to say, he thought. But he don't have to see Harpo in the street every day. And Angel and all them freaks. He wants to tell me what to do, let him try living on my block awhile. I dunno . . . I dunno . . .

I better think about the Nielsen Galleries, 'cause this other stuff's gonna drive me crazy. . . . I wonder what his face'll look like when he sees his paintings hanging there. That's one pretty great gallery I got him! If I can do this, I swear I can do anything! I don't need those freaks! They can take their gang and shove it!

Ramon avoided Madison Avenue until the very end of their trip, to keep Glasser from guessing what the surprise was. As they approached the Nielsen Galleries, Ramon crossed to the far side of the street, then wheeled across to the Galleries in the middle of the block.

"Watch out!" called Glasser. "They'll arrest you for jaywalking. Or I should say jaymushing!"

"Hey, Glasser, look at that!" said Ramon.

In the window, next to the Shahn painting, was a green-and-blue canvas by Arnold Glasser. The painting revealed depths of color in the October sunlight, a tidal pool of hidden shades.

Glasser stared for a moment. Then he rapped on the arm of the wheelchair. "Push me inside" was all he said.

On a wall near the entrance were four more of Glasser's paintings, each in a modern silver frame. A white card read:

ARNOLD GLASSER, AMERICAN,
UNTITLED WORKS, OIL ON CANVAS.

As Mr. Nielsen started walking toward them from the rear room, Glasser said sharply to Ramon, "Let go the wheelchair!" In a sudden plunge, he wheeled toward the paintings, reached up and tore one off the wall, then angrily hurled the canvas out toward the street.

He's gone crazy, thought Ramon. Crazy!

Ramon tried to hold his arm, but Glasser was too powerful. He pulled a second painting from the wall and hurled it to the floor.

"Glasser! What in hell are you doing!" Nielsen shouted. "GLASSER!"

"Take them down! Take them down! You have no right!"

"Glasser, come on! You know me! We'll sign a contract! We'll—"

"No contract! Nothing! I don't need your charity, Nielsen! Your reviews of my work back then were enough! More than enough! I don't need your charity!"

Ramon leaped in front of the third painting as Glasser moved toward it. There were needles of pain from the stitches in his neck. "Hey Glasser!" he called. "I done all this for you! What the hell are you doing! This ain't charity! What are you doing?"

"Get out of my way!" Glasser shouted shrilly.

"No! You're crazy! I got this gallery! I got you this! You can't do this to me! You can't! You—you can't!"

He knew his voice was breaking, but he didn't care. He pressed against the painting to keep Glasser away.

"I can't do this to *you*?" Glasser shouted to Ramon. "What about *me*? I also have my style! My pride! You're not the only one! . . . And *you*! You with your knife! With your revenge! With your gang war! You talk to me about doing something to you? What are you doing to yourself!"

"You were famous! You're a terrific painter! This ain't charity. Tell him, mister! Tell him!"

"*What*, tell me! Nielsen here, he hates my work! And he knows that nobody out there's ever heard of me! No one! It's charity!"

"No," said Nielsen calmly. "There's a real interest again in artists of the thirties—"

"Thirties! I didn't paint that garbage in the thirties! I painted it last month!"

Nielsen tried to answer, "Yes, but—"

"No buts!"

"Hey Glasser, who cares when you painted them!" said Ramon. "Your paintings are good. They're as good as any of the other stuff in this place. It's like

174

you wanna kill yourself all over again. It's like when you asked me to knife you. You wanna be dead! But these paintings, they make you alive! And they're better 'cause they're from now! These paintings, like—like, they're young. Please! Leave them up! Please!"

Glasser sat quietly thinking, while Nielsen watched uncertainly, not daring to say a word. Glasser, deep in thought, seemed to be talking to himself, his lips moving slightly. Then he shook his head. "No. No paintings. I have my style, just as you have yours. You see! I'm no different than you."

"Oh yes you are, man! You're scared! And I ain't!"

"Scared? Me? I'm not afraid of anything anymore."

"Oh yes you are! You're afraid to leave your paintings up! 'Cause maybe—maybe you think people will laugh or something! Or compare you against Pedro Picasso or something! You're scared, that's what! You'd rather sit in that room of yours with the lights out! You'd rather be dead! 'Cause you're scared to be alive!"

"So are you, punk!"

"Me? I am not! I'll take on anybody, one on one! I ain't scared of nothing!"

"Oh really! And how about *none* on one! You're afraid to *not* fight! You're afraid to give up that knife! What would they call you? A sissy? Weird? Like that friend of yours? You're the one who's afraid of people laughing at *you*! You're afraid of being your own self! *You're* scared, not me!"

Ramon and Glasser stared at each other, not saying a word. Nielsen moved gingerly toward a painting to pick it up off the floor, hesitated, then stopped. Slowly, Ramon put his hand in his right pocket and drew out his knife. He flicked it open, then closed it. Then he flicked it open and closed it, once more. The knife's tiny click filled the silent room, a click as familiar to him as the jump of his own pulse. He clutched the knife as if it were a hand. Then he reached out and dropped it into Glasser's lap.

"OK, Glasser . . . OK, man . . . I'll trade you. My scared for your scared. Even though I ain't scared! . . . But I'll trade you. . . . Is it a deal?"

Glasser examined the knife, then stared at Ramon again. He nodded his head slowly. "OK, wise guy . . . it's a deal. . . . Please hang my paintings, again, Nielsen. I've just transacted a swap. . . . My apologies."

"No apology needed," said Nielsen as he started to retrieve the canvases on the floor. "I'll prepare a contract—"

"We don't need a contract," said Glasser. "I know you, Nielsen. I know you. Take whatever commission you think is fair, *if* you sell any, which I doubt."

"Wait!" Ramon shouted. "You got my knife, right! You didn't get no *if* knife. You got my *real* knife! So don't give me no *if* he sells one. We're trading *real* stuff, not *if* stuff! It's like you're still trying to say your paintings are garbage. He will sell one! He will! You say that, man! Or the deal's off! He *will!*"

"Hmm . . . The point is well taken. Well taken. . . . He will!"

"That's better!" said Ramon. " 'Cause I ain't gonna walk around on them streets without a knife for *fun!*"

"All right. Enough," Glasser said. "Let's get out of here before I change my mind or you change yours. Or Nielsen has us both arrested. Come on. We'll go down to the Museum of Modern Art. It's not far."

"Yeah, I know that place," said Ramon. "That's just down the block from where I sold your paintings."

"I have news for you. That museum happens to own six of my paintings. You didn't know that, did you! They're in storage, but they bought them years ago. And you were selling them around the corner for twenty dollars. What do you think of that!"

"Hey! That's good. That's great!"

"What! Why?"

" 'Cause that's the first time I ever heard you show off, Glasser."

24

The day went quickly. At the Museum of Modern Art, there were works by Picasso that reminded Ramon of Glasser's delicate paintings, and others even stranger than the Picasso painting at the Nielsen Galleries. Picasso seemed to paint in a dozen different ways. But which was really him? Ramon wondered. Maybe I could write as many ways as Picasso painted. Or even more.

Afterward, they had sodas in the museum's sculpture garden. From the metal table where they sat, Ramon could see sleek curving shapes of iron and bronze, an enormous sculpture of a woman who looked as powerful as an Amazon, and another of a man who looked like the devil in disguise.

"That's Balzac," said Glasser, following Ramon's eyes. "One of Rodin's most famous sculptures. Do you like it?"

"Naa. It stinks. No place for little kids to climb up on it," said Ramon.

"Still being smart, hey?"

"Yeah, I gotta be, now that I ain't got no knife."

"Good. Then I can be stupid. Because now I *do* have a knife."

"I'll teach you how to use it."

"Thank you, but no thank you."

After the museum, as they went north through Central Park on the way back to Glasser's apartment, Ramon wheeled Glasser over to a group of teenagers with guitars playing Latin music.

"Listen to that beat," Ramon said. "Latino! That's modern art, too!"

"Of course it is," Glasser answered. "You think I understand only what's in museums, don't you? Well you're wrong. The best art is living art. Those kids over there are good!"

As they continued toward the West Side, Glasser started humming a complicated melody. "Mozart," he said. "That's living art, too. Next week maybe we'll go to a concert. . . ."

Glasser continued humming all the way to his apartment. Oh mama, thought Ramon, he sure paints better than he sings.

That evening, on the way back to his own apartment, Ramon saw Harpo in the street. He reached for his knife instinctively, but his pocket was empty. For a moment he felt a flurry of panic. I'm naked, he thought. He can cut me in half! Why'd I give

Glasser my knife? I gotta be crazy!

Then their eyes met, and Harpo looked down as he hurried past. It was clear. Harpo wouldn't bother him anymore. There'd been no victory, no honor, no macho, not with four against one.

He felt free. Free of them.

A sudden thought made Ramon stop walking. He gave a low whistle. Someday, he knew it, someday he'd write about Harpo. About all of them. It seemed to him, at that moment, as real and true as the broken pavement under his feet.

Those freaks!

Ramon climbed the two rickety flights to his apartment. It was still early. He could clean up the place some more, then go to the hospital—

But something was wrong. His door was unlocked. Maybe he'd been mistaken; maybe he wasn't free. Maybe the gang had gotten into his apartment and . . .

And the lights were on. The power had been turned back on. There was *salsa* music on the radio, and a familiar voice humming. His father's voice. It couldn't be!

Ramon walked slowly into the living room. His father was seated at the table looking through papers and bills, through all the accumulated wreckage of letters and warnings and notices.

Ramon started toward him, then held back. He had learned to hold back in the years of shouting.

"*Papi* . . . You're home. . . ."

His father looked up. "Ramon! Hey, look at you! Look at you!" he said in Spanish. "Tall! You're tall!"

"Hey, *papi* . . . how did you escape?" Ramon asked in English.

"No escape," his father answered in English. "I don't escape. You think I'm *loco*? I have parole. Parole, *comprendes*?"

"Hey? Hey, that's great! . . . *Mami*, she's in the hospital."

"I've seen her," Ramon's father said in Spanish. "Not so good, yet. It's going to take a few more weeks, the doctor said. . . . Hey, Ramon! We're going to fix up this place for her. Yes?"

"Yeah! I started already. I cleaned out the refrigerator and I washed the linoleum and I—"

"Wait! Say in Spanish. You talk *inglés* too fast."

"I've been cleaning up," said Ramon in Spanish. "The kitchen was full of roaches."

"I'll get powder. We'll put down powder. . . . What's that picture over your bed, hey? That's some funny kind of picture."

"It's a painting. A . . . a friend of mine painted it."

"Ah ha! You have some fancy friends now, eh? That queer, Felipe, did he paint it? I don't want you hanging around with a queer like him," his father said in Spanish.

Ramon struggled to hold in his anger. "Felipe

isn't queer," he answered carefully in Spanish. "But even if he is, I don't care. He's my friend."

"Some friend!"

"Anyway, that painting isn't his. It's a present from . . . someone."

"Ah ha! I see! I see! You got a girl friend, eh? Hey, you can tell your father all about—"

"He's a painter. A famous painter. He's got pictures in museums, and on the walls of colleges, and everything."

"What painter?"

"He's a very old guy. He used to be famous, and he's going to be famous again. He's in a wheelchair, but he can still paint."

"How did you get mixed up with some old bum like that?"

Talk about something else, thought Ramon. "Hey, papi, don't get mad. But could you tell me, you know, what it was like where you were? In Attica?"

"It's bad! That's all I'm going to say! Don't ask me any more! Never! . . . But you don't have to worry. I'm not mad. I'm not getting angry anymore. No more. It's a new me. Your mama, I told her at the hospital. No more anger. No more temper. Never . . . Say, Ramon, what's all that tape on your neck there?" Ramon's father pointed at the bandages.

"Oh . . . a fight. . . . Nothing. . . . I got cut, that's all."

"Who won?"

"Me."

"With honor?"

"Yes."

Was he lying? No . . . Harpo had looked down. But he hadn't won. He *was* lying. Lying so his father would leave him alone.

"Good. To win a fight honorably, that's being a man. I'm proud of you."

Ramon turned away; he couldn't look into his father's eyes. Tell him the truth, he thought. Who cares what he thinks? Who cares who won? Tell him now. Tell him!

"Papi . . . uh . . . I didn't win. It was four against one . . . but I didn't win," he said softly in Spanish.

"Then why did you say you won! Hey? Why?"

"Because . . . I don't know. . . ."

"Why! I'm not home for a year, I see you for ten minutes, and you're lying to me! Why?"

"Because I'm never all right the way I am! You want me always to win! To be macho! *I'm not macho!*"

Ramon's father seemed dazed by his outburst. He tried to calm Ramon. "Four against one is honorable. You don't have to win against four. You don't—"

"I don't have to win against anybody! I can be honorable and lose! I don't have a knife anymore! I'm not fighting anymore! So call me anything you want! 'Cause I'm gonna be macho *my* way, not your way!"

183

Ramon rushed to the bathroom to escape. In the bathroom, behind the locked door, he could think. He heard his father's voice from the living room.

"You always give me headaches! You're taller, but you're the same! The same!"

Ramon shut his ears. I ain't the same, he thought. *He's* the same, not me! Let him shout. That's outside of me. Inside me, that's where I am! Inside!

"Ramon!"

They can all shout. I don't care. Nobody's gonna tell me what to be. Not *him*. Not Harpo. Not Glasser. Nobody. I'm gonna be me, from inside. Like Felipe. Yeah, I made up my mind.

"Come out here! Ramon!"

Maybe I'll go to school. And maybe I won't. Maybe I'll really write. And maybe I won't. Maybe I'll even paint. Or sell paintings. Or join *papá* in that Puerto Rico stuff. Or maybe I won't. But it's gonna be me, man. Me!

"Don't you hear me! I'm talking to you!" his father shouted.

Seated on the closed toilet, Ramon took the book from his pocket and wrote rapidly:

October 10.
Ramon Santiago! That's me! With two knife cuts on me. Roaches in the kitchen. A Puerto Rican face. And a brain half made of air. And anybody don't like it can shove it good!